Strauser, Eddy, and Jason

Taken from the Book

"Stories from the Devil's Den"

A pair of stories by John Baniszewski

Dedication

To Daniel, Beth, the Turkey Bowl Gang, and especially, to Helen.

Acknowledgment

I would like to acknowledge the 160,000 soldiers who suffered so greatly during the horrific battle at Gettysburg, especially the 10,000 whose lives ended there. I also wish to acknowledge the tens of thousands of grieving parents, widows, and orphans of those soldiers. I am grateful to those veterans of the battle who, in the 1880's, purchased land and commissioned the building of hundreds of monuments that tell the stories of the friends they forever left behind at Gettysburg. I am grateful for the gift those veterans presented to our federal government in 1895, when they transferred ownership of their 500 acres to the US War Department. Without that gift, there would be no national park here today. I am grateful to the government people, the civil servants, who maintain the park, and allow us to see the battlefield as the soldiers saw it. Having been one for 35 years, I know how underappreciated civil servants can be, and how they are often not given the resources needed to do their job to the best of their abilities and desires.

I want to thank Mom and Dad (Irene and Joe), who took me to Fort Niagara when I was a little boy, igniting my love of history, and where I heard the first "supernatural" story about slain soldiers. I especially thank Mom for nagging Dad to finally make that trip to visit Washington DC, and for taking the side trip on the way back to Erie, allowing me to visit the battlefield for the first time, on the

100th anniversary of the battle (1963). I still have a photo of me, age 12, standing atop the Devil's Den, which I found to be the most fascinating part of the battlefield.

I want to thank my former NASA co-worker Rick – during the tour I gave for our management team, after I finished narrating the battle-related events at the Devil's Den, he asked me "Do you know any ghost stories?" I quickly made one up on the spot. But for some reason, when I got home that day, I decided to put that story on paper, and improve it. For reasons I do not know, after I finished that story, I wrote another, and then another, and another, finally quitting at twelve. I also want to thank my "Turkey Bowl" buddies, some of whom read my book, and especially my good buddy Bill (a former editor for the Erie Times-News) who said "John, you should publish this!" Bill knows how to write.

I wish to thank my fellow Licensed Battlefield Guides (LBG), who share my love of the battlefield, and who have shown me some good story-telling tricks. A visit to Gettysburg is incomplete if you do not hire one of us to guide you through the battlefield, and to tell you the amazing true stories that you would never learn on your own. I hope they will forgive me for writing a book involving ghosts.

I wish to thank the 15,000 or so folks who allowed me to take them around the battlefield during the past 24 years, enabling me to hone my story-telling skills, and who gave me confidence that I know how to tell a story.

I want to thank my friends who were my "guinea pigs" when I was preparing for the extremely challenging task of passing the incredibly difficult tests that one must take to become an LBG. I want to thank my wonderful kids, Beth and Daniel, who put up with my Gettysburg infatuation.

My greatest thanks go to my wonderful wife Helen. Had I not met her, I might not be living in Gettysburg, in a lovely house that borders the battlefield. Every time when I came home after a day of doing tours, she immediately asked me "How were your tours today? How were your customers? Did they ask any good questions?" She would be my helper during the all-day "Lessons of Leadership from The Battle of Gettysburg" training programs that I occasionally conducted. I lost her in 2023 after a too-short marriage (cancer sucks!). I miss her enthusiasm and her wonderful laugh.

Contents

The Spirit of the Devil's Den – Another Origin

"That man whom your outward form reveals is not yourself. The spirit is the true self, not that physical figure which can be pointed out by your finger" – Cicero, Roman orator, & politician.

At the south end of the Gettysburg battlefield is an eerie formation of enormous boulders, balanced in precarious ways, riven with crevices, and surrounded by dark forests and towering hills. This place is named the Devil's Den. If you seek to find a spirit, here you may find one. But it is one you may not wish to find.

Places may have a spirit. In some places, these spirits can speak to us in ways we do not fully understand. We sometimes give names to these places. The Wailing Wall…Calvary…Omaha Beach…Dealey Plaza…Ground Zero.

There is such a place in south-central Pennsylvania. We name it Gettysburg. At that place, in the summer of 1863, tens of thousands of young Americans experienced a horror unmatched in America's history, a horror that can still be sensed today.

A Gettysburg veteran named Joshua Chamberlain said, *"On great fields…spirits linger"*. He talked of the spirits associated with the great Battle of 1863. But there is one spirit that inhabited this place for centuries before the Battle of Gettysburg – namely, the Spirit of the Devil's Den.

In 1966, a show titled "Star Trek" debuted on television. It was set in a distant future when humanity had invented space ships that could travel faster than light. Humans encountered hundreds of worlds in which there was intelligent life, and Earth and many of these worlds formed a federation of planets. The show was set aboard a "starship" named Enterprise. The captain, named Kirk, was born in Iowa. His second-in-command, whose name was Spock, was born on a planet named Vulcan, and among the people of Vulcan, logic was valued highly, and emotion was discouraged. Spock once said to Kirk, "We have a saying on Vulcan – Only Nixon Could Go to China."

In 1972, Nixon was the President of the United States. For his entire life, he constantly proclaimed that Communism, as a form of government, was monstrous and that the United States must oppose Communism everywhere it existed. To the great shock of millions of people, he traveled to China to meet with their highest leader. Those who admire Nixon say this was an act of greatness. His years of condemning communism gave him the ability to discuss peace with communist leaders.

In 1972, the United States was a great military and economic power. The communist nation of China was rapidly growing, and it was clear that in the near future, China would also become a great military and economic power. In the first half of the 20th Century, several nations that were great powers fought two wars in which 100,000,000 people died. Those who admire Nixon say that because of Nixon's visit, he may have prevented a future war between the United States and China. The two nations would become rivals but not enemies. One thousand years earlier, there was a person who attempted to do what Nixon would do in the 20th Century. She failed. Her name was Dawn.

The people who inhabited the North American continent comprised many nations. The rock formation that is today called the Devil's Den was on the border of two of those nations. The borders of these nations were not clearly defined, but each nation believed that certain lands should belong only to them, as those lands contained the wild animals that were hunted for food.

The nation to the north stretched all the way to the enormous body of water we today call Lake Erie. The nation to the south stretched all the way to the enormous body of water we today call the Chesapeake Bay.

These two nations had both similarities and differences. Their languages are not alike. Both also believed that the strange rock formation we call the Devil's Den was a sacred place created by their God for a mysterious and unknown purpose. On occasions, the two nations would fight each other in order to gain complete control of the Devil's Den.

***

As the war party returned, Dawn looked for faces. Too many were missing. She knew all of their faces. She had been the midwife for almost all of them. This was the third time in the last seven years that she watched a ravaged war party return. She made a decision.

After a day of rest, the leader of the war party spoke to the entire village. He related how, when they arrived at the place of the sacred stones, they were surprised that a war party from the Northern nation was already there. Worse, they had never imagined the Northern nation could assemble such a large war party. The leader said that as soon as they were spotted, their enemy attacked, and it was clear that because of the great numbers of the enemy, standing and fighting would mean certain death. A dozen of the bravest warriors sacrificed themselves, fighting as long as they could, holding their ground long enough for the other warriors to make an escape. Not one of those dozen survived. Their enemy kept pursuing them, but not for very long. Their enemy seemed satisfied with the quick victory they had achieved.

Immediately, there were calls for blood, many warriors urging that a greater war party set out tomorrow, and many grieving parents demanding that their sons be avenged. "I must let their boiling blood rage for a while," thought Dawn. Emotions were too high. "Tomorrow, the elders will meet," she thought. That is when she would exert her will. As the most respected of the elders, she was certain that her decision would be accepted. That acceptance, she knew, would not come easily. But come it will, she decided. She made an oath to herself. In her many years she had never broken such an oath.

The meeting of the elders began at sunset the next day. Immediately, there were calls to create the next war party, angry demands for revenge, and calls for the spilling of the enemy's blood. But less than two minutes after the meeting began, the gathered elders were startled by the shout of a powerful voice, a voice unlike that ever heard before in this room, a shout demanding "Silence!" Every eye was now turned upon Dawn. This had never happened. Never had Dawn spoken so soon after the beginning of a meeting, and never had she spoken so powerfully. In every meeting of the elders, she would sit silently, listening raptly, hearing every argument, never interrupting debate. At those meetings, though, when she finally did speak. the words that she spoke were always wise and insightful. It was clear that every word she spoke was deliberate, words that came from many years of observing every aspect of village life. What she would say today, however, was unprecedented.

"There will be no more debate! There will be no arguing! I have made a decision. I have determined what must be done. I have seen too much death. I refuse to see more! Tomorrow, at sunset, the entire village will gather. I will speak to everyone. This meeting is finished! Return to your homes!" With that, she walked from the chamber. For several minutes, every person in that chamber was silent. A group of people who had always argued and debated were stunned that Dawn had spoken so forcefully and with such authority. Had any other elder attempted what Dawn had done, there would have been no chance of success. Dawn had counted on that respect which she had so rightfully earned. The silent group of elders quietly left the chamber, each of them wondering what Dawn would say the next day.

The following night, every eye was upon Dawn, and every mouth was hushed in anticipation. She stood before the crowd and, for two minutes, was silent. She then spoke with a powerful voice heard clearly by every villager. "I have seen too much death!" she roared. "I have decided what must be done. If you do not like my decision, that will not concern me. If you want to debate my decision, that will be fruitless. I would like for some help, but if no one offers to help, I will act upon my decision". Dawn spoke with such decisiveness that not one person made a sound.

"I will travel to the Northern nation. They have a person who is to them as I am to you. I will go to the village of that person. I will go to talk to him. For now, that is all I will do. He and I will talk. I wish to be accompanied by four warriors. Only four. The warriors will leave their weapons behind. I now call upon you, warriors. If you will come with me, step forward. But if none of you step forward, I will go alone. No one will prevent me from going". Immediately, there was startled discussion among the villagers, cries of surprise, and shouts of objection, but within seconds, Dawn's great voice again silenced the crowd. "There will be no debate. Quiet your voices! If there is a warrior will to do as I request, step forward". All eyes turned toward the warrior group that stood at the edge of the crowd. After a minute, one warrior stepped forward, shouting, "I will go!" Soon, a second stepped forward, shouting the same oath. Two more then stepped forward. "That is enough!" Dawn loudly decreed. "Come forward, stand before me. The four warriors did as ordered.

"I do not know where the person I must speak to is located. Their nation is large. I need the four of you to precede me. You must travel to their nation, find that person, and tell him that I will visit him and that we will talk. Tell him that is all we will do. We will talk. If he objects to my coming, tell him that I will come anyway. You will bring no weapons with you on this journey. You will leave the day following tomorrow. You must complete your task as fast as you can. I now ask the four of you if you are willing to perform this task". It took her a minute for them to answer. The four talked among themselves, talking in low voices unheard by the crowd. The four turned to dawn and, as one voice, all four declared, "We will go."

The four warriors began their journey at the time appointed. The next few weeks were a time of anxiety for the village. There were many who declared that Dawn was a fool, that she was sending these four warriors on a fool's errand, and probably to certain death. Some argued that she had become too old, that her days of wisdom had ended, and that she was afflicted with the diminishing faculties that sometimes accompany old age. But the doubts about Dawn's wisdom were assuaged much sooner than anyone had imagined. The four returned, unharmed, in far fewer days than anyone thought possible. The message they delivered brought relief to Dawn. She was told that her counterpart would talk with her. He made a promise that her travel to his village would be safe.

At the start of the second full moon, Dawn stood before the man who was her counterpart. His name was Setting Moon. He looked her in the eye and spoke four words. Standing beside him was a young woman. "I was born in your nation," the young woman said to Dawn, who was amazed that the woman spoke in Dawn's tongue. The young woman gave an explanation. "I was not born in your village," the woman narrated, "but that is why I know your tongue. When I was a girl, I traveled with my parents on a pilgrimage to this place. But my father unknowingly stepped on the cub of a bear, not knowing the bear's mother was nearby. The bear rushed at him and slashed his throat with its great claw. The bear then ran at my mother, who screamed to me, "Run!" I will never see my mother again. I ran and ran and ran as fast as I could until I collapsed. I did not know where I was. I wandered for days. I had no food. I eventually fell to the earth, expecting that I would pass on to the home of our spirits. But a woman of this nation, a woman of a gathering party, came upon me. She fed me and took me to her home. I became her daughter. When Setting Moon speaks to you, I will tell you what he says, and you will tell me what to say to him. Setting Moon says that only the three of us will talk. We will talk until we have said all that needs to be said. He has already spoken to you. What he said to you was, 'You are very brave'". With that, the woman led Dawn to the tent, accompanied by Setting Moon.

To everyone's surprise, they talked for four days. At the end of the fourth day, Dawn said to her four warriors, "Tomorrow at dawn, we return home. I will not speak until we are home. I will then speak to all of our people." True to her word, she said nothing during the journey.

There was great anticipation among the people as Dawn took her place on the speaking platform. Again, she spoke with authority and clarity. "Setting Moon and I agreed that too many have died. Both nations revere the place of the great stones. He and I have agreed that it belongs to both of our nations. Anyone from either nation may visit there safely. Never again will violence occur at that place. He and I have taken an oath to each other. But that is not enough. Each of us, each person of both nations, must take that same oath. And the taking of that oath must be seen by our gods. That oath must be taken at the sacred place of the stones."

There was surprise among the crowd. Immediately, people began expressing startlement, shock, anger, and fear, but in seconds, Dawn silenced the crowd with a gesture. "We shall leave in seven days," she directed the people. "Use that time to prepare. Any person who can make the journey must come, even if you are very old very young, or very weak. I have no more to say. Return to your homes, and prepare!" With that, Dawn descended from the platform and walked toward her home.

The coming days were not just days of preparation. These were days of debate, of arguments, days in which it was clear that many were convinced that Dawn was wrong, that peace between the two nations was impossible, and that only the people of the Southern nation should be allowed to visit the place of sacred stones. People sometimes screamed at each other, called each other fools, and sometimes even threatened each other. Many felt that Dawn had no right to make such a decision without the people having a say, for the village had always made difficult decisions by a vote, but only after there had been enough time for every opinion to be heard and debated. There was clearly no unanimity among the people. Many, but not most, were opposed, and some were very strongly opposed. Those most passionate were many warriors, the people who had engaged so often in battle against that foreign nation. These were the ones who had seen comrades die at the hands of their enemy, who had seen the savagery and cruelty of the enemy warriors. These were the ones who most wanted revenge, not a treaty of peace.

A cycle of the moon later, a great crowd assembled at the place of the great stones. Many were seeing this place for the first time, and the enormity of the rocks, the way in which they were piled and balanced, and the ominous darkness of the crevasses and small caves created a sense of awe and fear. Dawn and Setting Moon stood atop a flat boulder, one with a concave surface, a rock sometimes called the Gods' Table. The two leaders called for silence, each saying the same words but in their own tongues, taking turns to speak. Each leader held a sack made from animal stomachs. Dawn spoke first. "We have come here to take an oath," she declared, "an oath that this place shall belong to both of our nations, that all may come here in safety, that from now on, there shall be no violence at this place." When Setting Moon was done, Dawn again spoke. "I hold the sacred water of our bay. Setting Moon holds the water of his great lake. We shall pour the waters into the bowl at our feet so the waters mingle. As we pour the water, this is what all of you must say so that the spirits that reside in this place can hear our oath." When Setting Moon concluded, Dawn again instructed her people, "These are the words you will speak. You will say, 'This place belongs to both our nations. We shall never commit violence at this place'". When Setting Moon was done, the two leaders held the sacks of water up for the people to see. At that moment, a warrior of the Southern nation sprang from the crowd and flung a spear. That spear struck Dawn in her chest. An archer from the southern nation sprang from the crowd and shot an arrow that hit Setting Moon in the throat.

The peacemaker's Dawn and Setting Moon believed that spirits inhabited the Devil's Den. They knew little of these spirits, but they assumed the spirits were benign. What they did not know was that the spirit there had been conceived years before, conceived when an innocent woman was cruelly murdered and her blood poured by her murderer into the basin of the Gods' Stone. The evil spirit was formed from the blood of the woman and the hatred of her murderer. Because the spirit was of hate, it could sense hate. The spirit somehow knew that among the two nations, there was disagreement and anger within the nations. The spirit had the power to turn disagreement into anger, to turn anger into hate, a hate so great that the eyes of its victims could see only blind rage.

A warrior of the southern nation had slain the leader of his own nation. A similar warrior of the Northern nation had slain the Northern leader. Several warriors of the Southern nation attacked the Southern man who had thrown the spear, but some of his Southern comrades came to his defense. The same occurred among the Northerners. The hatred of these warriors spread like a plague to the hunters, to the farmers, to the young, and to the old. Many grabbed the abundant stones from the ground and used them as weapons. Northern brother and sister slew Northern sister and brother. Southern mothers attacked their own sons, and northern men attacked their own fathers. By the end of the day, none moved. In a way, the oath was obeyed. No Southerner killed a Southerner, and no Northerner killed a Northerner.

On July 2, 1863, the second day of the Battle of Gettysburg, different men fought and killed each other by the hundreds on the very rocks of the Devil's Den, staining the boulders red. By day's end, the land around the Devil's Den was once more saturated with human blood.

The Spirit attained the height of its power on July 2, 1863. Most of its victims were soldiers who were in its realm during the battle. But the end of the War did not mean the end of the Spirit nor the end of its malevolence. Those who would live for ages to come were neither safe nor immune.

Strauser – An Introduction

After the Civil war ended, the United States of America enjoyed enormous growth. New technologies and new inventions resulted in the building of factories, especially in the northern states. The flood of immigrants grew, many of whom were poor and futureless in their home countries, and the new factories were often filled with these wretched refugees. They would do the dirtiest and most dangerous work and would work for pennies but still be better off than if they had not come to America.

It was the great and speedy iron machines, the railroads that traveled on tracks of steel, that tied the country together and allowed growth to spread. Few people were better than Strauser at building railroads. A key to his success was his ability to always be the low bidder. Those immigrants were the wards of his key. He used immigrants like a steam locomotive used coal. Using a shovel, the fireman would scoop up lumps of coal and toss them into the firebox. The faster they burned, the hotter the coal-fueled fire got, and the train reached its destination faster. Eventually, someone would remove the ashes, all that was left of the coal.

Another aspect of Strauser's success was his ability to meet deadlines. If he was given a schedule to meet, he always met it. Nothing could stand in his way once his goal was set. Nothing!

As fast as money came to Strauser, the faster he spent it in gambling bars, brothels, luxury hotels, and five-star restaurants. He needed a new income stream. He found one at Gettysburg. He did not know it was a deep and deadly stream.

The Trolley

When the carnage ended, the opposing armies marched away to spill their blood on other distant battlefields. For a few years, the land around the Devil's Den was peaceful, and the evil Spirit that resided there lay dormant.

But men came again, hosts of men bent on destruction. This time, the men did not attack each other. They attacked the land of the Devil's Den itself.

Hundreds of men wielded axes to fell the trees around the Den. They gashed the earth itself with shovels and machines. Boulders that had withstood the ravages of nature for millions of years were blown to fragments by charges of black powder. The men who attacked the land did not know of the power of the Spirit that lived there. Some would soon learn.

There are people who look at the fields and hillsides of the Gettysburg battlefield and see the hallowed ground. There are people who look at the same fields and hillsides and see a chance to make money. Strauser was one of the latter.

Mr. Strauser sat in the ornate lobby of his Philadelphia hotel, finishing a sumptuous breakfast. As he ate, he studied his newspaper intently, looking for an opportunity. He needed one.

When he arrived in town two months ago, his bank account was full of money. Thanks to his gambling bills and a taste for fine living, that was no longer the case. It was time to get back to work.

Strauser always came back to Philadelphia. After all, it was his hometown. Although he had spent little time there the past several years, he never lost his fondness for the city. He enjoyed its fine restaurants and hotels. He made good use of its excellent newspapers. Strauser felt pity for the foolish men who looked for gold in the God-forsaken deserts out west. He found gold in the newspapers.

First, he scanned the advertising section, but he found nothing of note. He turned to the news section and then to the editorials, reading these sections thoroughly and carefully.

He paid special attention to anything that dealt with railroads. After all, railroads had been good to him, and he, in turn, had been good to them. In the last few decades, the railroad industry grew enormously in this country, and many men made a great deal of money from them, including Strauser. There was no reason to think this boom wouldn't continue in 1893.

Strauser had no interest in managing railroads, and he was too impatient to invest in them. He liked to build them. Strauser had a specialty – he helped railroads that were in trouble.

Several times in the past decade, Strauser matched himself up with railroads that were having problems completing new rail lines. Railroads were enormously expensive to build. The investors who put up the money were very unhappy with any rail company that promised to build new lines but did not finish them as scheduled. After all, time was money!

The labor crews who built the rail lines were becoming more of a problem all the time. Despite the advances in technology made in the late nineteenth century, railroads still depended upon massive gangs of crude, illiterate laborers working with shovels and, hammers, and muscle. Their wages cost a fortune, and they always demanded more! With all the troublemakers going around trying to organize the workers into mobs called "unions," labor crews were becoming impossible to deal with. Strauser, however, knew how to deal with them.

Strauser developed a reputation in the railroad industry as a man who got things done. If a new rail line was behind schedule and over its budget, Strauser could fix that problem. There was more than one railroad executive who had saved his own high-paying job because he had the intelligence to hire Strauser. He did not work cheap, but he was worth every penny.

When Strauser took over a construction crew, productivity increased enormously. Work did not stop when it rained or snowed. If one man had an accident, Strauser made sure that the other men pressed on. Injured workers were replaced rapidly and with little disruption. Union organizers never seemed to stay long around Strauser's crews. Indeed, in recent years, several railroad owners have come to love Strauser. Hundreds of workers learned to hate him.

Once again, from the comfort of his hotel, Strauser looked for a railroad that needed him. He would offer them his services, and he would fix their problems. Then, he would allow them to replenish his depleted bank account.

So far, his hunt through the newspaper has yielded no fruit. There were ads by the Baltimore & Ohio and the Pennsylvania Railroads looking for men. These offered nothing out of the ordinary. The news pages were also unproductive. In fact, there was hardly a story about railroads to be found.

He perused the editorials, finding nothing of promise there either. But as he was about to turn the page, something caught his eye. "Another Battle in Gettysburg," the headline read. He started reading.

The first few paragraphs were quite dull. There were several quotes from members of the Union Army Veterans Group, the Grand Army of the Republic. These men were tossing out words like "desecration" and "national disgrace." But then he saw the words he was looking for. "Lawsuit." "Court order". This was promising!

Apparently, a company was attempting to build a trolley line through the Gettysburg battlefield. They were opposed by a number of groups whom the newspaper dubbed "preservationists." These groups were pursuing various legal actions, including injunctions, in an effort to halt construction. Evidently, feelings ran high among a great many people. "I imagine the trolley company is eager to get their line finished before someone stops them," Strauser thought. "Perhaps I should pay them a visit."

"Never worked on a trolley before," he said to himself, "but it can't be all that different from a railroad." He went to the telegraph office to send discreet inquiries to a number of his associates. By the next day, he had the name of the man to contact - Mr. Edward Hoffer, president and principal financier of the Gettysburg Electric Railway. He sent a letter to Mr. Hoffer, including several glowing recommendations from selected former employers. A few days later, he received a reply. Mr. Hoffer would like to meet with him in Gettysburg.

The following Monday, Strauser's train arrived at Gettysburg. He strolled from the train station to the town square. His train had been packed with aging Union veterans, traveling to Gettysburg for a number of different reunions. In the square, dozens of local entrepreneurs attempted to sell their services to the newly arrived visitors. Three different men approached Strauser, asking if he would like a private guided tour of the battlefield. Owners of numerous liveries solicited customers to rent carriages. "Indeed," observed Strauser, "it looks like a battlefield trolley could be a very profitable venture."

Strauser hired a guide, who asked him if there was any particular part of the battlefield that most interested him. The guide was surprised when Strauser said, "Show me the Trolley line." The guide said, "Well, usually I start with Day One of the battle, which is north and west of the town, and later we get to the Day Two area.."

The guide was shocked when Strauser shouted, "Just show me the trolley line, Damn it! I don't need to hear about the stupid battle! Let's go!"

Overall, Strauser was satisfied with the tour. He got an idea for the terrain. He could see that the trolley line could indeed be a success. There seemed to be plenty of tourists here. It irritated him that during the tour, the stupid guide kept trying to talk about the god-damned battle, but after Strauser put the guide in his place a few times, he shut his mouth and just followed Strauser's orders.

When his tour was done, he visited the hotel where he was to meet Mr. Hoffer and had dinner there. The following day, Strauser met Hoffer at the bar. The two got quickly down to business.

At first, Strauser let the other man talk. Hoffer rambled on about how unfair his situation was, about how he was only trying to bring a little much-needed prosperity to this backward Pennsylvania town. His trolley would certainly be a boon to all of the visiting veterans who came here with their families. After all, the battlefield was quite large, and these visitors had to travel miles from the town to visit the places where they fought. But there were always some fools who stood in the way of progress, Hoffer complained, short-sighted do-gooders obsessed with preserving every cow pasture and outhouse in the area. It wasn't as if the trolley line would harm anything of true historical value! And now he was squandering his valuable money to pay lawyers to fight injunctions. What a tremendous waste!

Hoffer seemed impressed by the letters of recommendation that Strauser gave him. Strauser spent some time embellishing his past accomplishments. Soon, the men were talking contract terms, and before long, they settled on a figure that Strauser had found quite fair. In fact, if Strauser met the ambitious schedules that Hoffer established, the contract provided incentive bonuses that were quite lucrative. The men parted, and Strauser booked a room in the hotel for an extended stay in Gettysburg.

On the first day on the job, Strauser inspected the construction site. He was appalled. The labor crew was no surprise - it was the usual collection of illiterate immigrants and other imported scum. What bothered Strauser was the leisurely pace that the foremen were permitting. He would soon change that.

He found the superintendent's shed. Strauser wanted to familiarize himself with every detail of the operation, and that's where the records would be. He sat down at the desk, which was carelessly strewn with papers. On top of the mess was a letter addressed to him. He read it and was somewhat surprised. It was from his predecessor, the man Hoffer had just fired. "What a noble fellow," Strauser thought, "so conscientious." The letter described the status of various aspects of the project and made recommendations concerning problems needing immediate attention. Strauser chuckled and threw the letter in the waste basket. He got to work.

It was not long before Strauser's managerial abilities made an impact on the construction operation. The land was cleared more quickly, and progress on grading the rail bed improved dramatically. The track was laid at a much faster pace. Accidents among the workers went up, but that was to be expected, and replacement labor was easy to find. Expenses for wages actually decreased. Strauser had some unexpected costs when he needed to hire a few men to deal with troublesome labor organizers, but he considered it money well spent. Strauser easily met the first of his deadlines and was quite pleased to deposit his hefty incentive bonus in the bank.

Weeks went by. Progress was still good but not as rapid as Strauser desired. He suspected there were troublemakers among the work crew, men who would like to sabotage his good efforts. He would need to root them out, and soon. He barely met his second bonus deadline.

On Thursday, he was at the superintendent's shed. He was in a foul mood. His rail supplier was late with delivery, and there had been a recent theft of shovels and other tools. Strauser also received a rude telegram the day before from Mr. Hoffer, reminding him that certain court proceedings were approaching and that progress needed to pick up.

He heard a knock at the door. He did not turn around. He merely snapped, "Who is it?" There was no answer. Angrily, he spun around. In the doorway stood Santini.

He disliked Santini and was sure the feeling was mutual. Santini was the oldest man on the crew, and the workers treated him as a leader. Santini did not cower like the others did. Strauser was sure Santini was a troublemaker, but so far, he had been unable to catch the man in an act that was grounds to fire him. He made a mental note to do so soon.

"What is it?" Strauser barked, "Why aren't you working?" "There is something you need to take a look at," Santini replied, "at the construction site." Strauser was not happy about the interruption, but there was something about the man's tone that told him he shouldn't say no. "Let's go," he snorted, grabbing his hat.

The two men walked to the site. It was a considerable distance. They did not talk. They arrived at the area in the woods where the construction crew was clearing and grading the land. He saw a dozen men with shovels and picks standing there, not digging. Strauser seethed. "Why the Devil, aren't you men at work?" he demanded. They said nothing. One man pointed at the ground.

He saw that the men had dug a shallow hole, a foot or two

deep, a dozen across. He walked closer and looked into the hole. It was full of bones, human bones. He counted half a dozen skulls. Strauser frowned and pondered for a couple of seconds. He turned to Santini. "Get Conlon over here!" he ordered.

Conlon was a clerk, one of the few locals who worked for the trolley company. He was also a veteran and had fought at Gettysburg. Conlon was also a bit of a historian. He had read many books about the battle, and he made some money in the summer giving tours.

In twenty minutes, Conlon arrived. Strauser pointed to the bones. "What do you make of this?" he demanded. Conlon gave out a whistle and then stepped into the shallow pit. For several minutes, he poked around the bones and searched the dirt. He picked up several small objects and showed them to Strauser. There was a rusted buckle and a few buttons.

"Looks like you found yourself some Rebels!" Conlon stated, "Texans, I figure, from the design on these buttons." Strauser's face looked blank as Conlon continued. "The second day of the battle, Robert E. Lee decided to have twenty-thousand of his boys take a crack at us. We turned them back, we did, but they were tough fighters. These fellas here were probably part of General Hood's Texas Brigade. They were the first ones to hit us."

He pointed east through the trees. There was a stone fence

visible, with a clearing on the far side. The land sloped upward to a ridge above. "Our boys was up top that ridge when they came charging at us. We charged right back and pushed them to that wall, but more Rebels came up, and the Texans attacked us again. Within an hour, that field was filled with bodies, both ours and theirs. These fellas evidently were among the unlucky ones."

"The burying details had a lot of work that night. They'd dig a shallow ditch, throw a man in, cover him up, and go on to the next one. Sometimes, if they could find a piece of wood, they would scratch the names of the dead on it and stick it near the grave".

"After the battle, old Governor Curtin bought some land on Cemetery Hill and made a decent resting place for our boys in what's now the national cemetery. It took a few months, but the Union dead were all dug up and reburied there. The Rebels, though, lay there for years. After the war, they dug them up, too, and sent them back South. The ones they couldn't identify got buried in Richmond somewhere".

"What happened to these men?" Santini asked. "Hard to say", Conlon replied. "The Rebels only held this ground a couple of days before old George Meade convinced Mr. Lee and his army to return to Virginia. If there was a marker with names on it, some Union soldier probably used it for firewood. A grave that's in the woods like this gets covered up by leaves in the fall. Within a year or two of the battle, you probably couldn't even tell there was a grave here. Looks like these Southern boys have been lying here forgotten for close to thirty years now".

The whole time Conlon spoke, Strauser said nothing. He looked deep in thought. When Conlon finished his explanation, he turned to Strauser. "Well, sir, if you like, I'll go see the folks at the Battle Monument Commission tomorrow morning and tell them what we found." Strauser looked puzzled. "Why would you do that?" he demanded.

"Well," Conlon replied, "they'll probably want to send someone out here to look around for some more clues as to these men's identities. They'll want to dig around to see if there's more of 'em buried nearby. If they can't figure out who they are, they'll want to send the bones to Richmond."

Strauser was not happy at the prospect. The process sounded like it would take time, and he didn't have time. His next deadline was coming up. He'd be damned if he'd let some fool preservationists hold up his trolley just for a bunch of bones.

Strauser pointed a finger at Conlon and spoke. "If you report a word about this to anyone, you will be fired immediately", he threatened. He turned to the work crew. "That goes for the rest of you, too," he warned. "Santini," Strauser barked, "tell the ones who don't speak English what I just said. Anyone who mentions this to anybody will deeply regret it. You have my word." The men knew he would keep that word. They remembered what he had done to the union organizers.

"Pile those bones up in one spot!" he ordered. Several men hesitated. Strauser swore at them and made angry threats. Reluctantly, the workmen gathered up the bones and heaped them in a pile. "Now get some sledge-hammers," he commanded. The men looked perplexed, but they did as they were told. He had the men surround the pile of bones.

"I want those bones smashed into powder," he commanded Santini. "I don't want to see one recognizable fragment. Do you understand me?" Santini looked at him coldly. He passed Strauser's instructions on to the men. Three of them refused to obey, and Strauser fired them on the spot. The others were intimidated, for they desperately needed their meager wages. They got to work.

Bones that had been splintered by lead bullets thirty years ago were again smashed, this time by iron hammers. Skulls that had rested peacefully underground for decades were pounded into powder. By the time the workmen finished, the mortal remains of those six Confederate soldiers were nothing but a pile of dust on the forest floor. Not a fragment was left that was bigger than a kernel of corn.

Strauser had them break out shovels. He ordered the dust and fragments to be scattered. The bits and pieces of bone were flung out among the trees and rocks. When the work was done there was no indication that this spot of ground had been the final resting place of six men.

By the time they finished, it was dark. Strauser allowed the men to go back to their camp. The next day, they were back at work, clearing more land and laying more track. Also, the next day, the accidents started to happen.

Accidents were common enough, but the cause was usually clear- a careless man, a shoddy piece of equipment breaking. These accidents were different.

In the first one, a huge tree limb crashed down suddenly on three men, one of whom was badly injured. When they inspected the branch and tree, they found no sign of rot or disease. The next day, a supply wagon caught fire, though there was nothing unusually combustible in it. Several hundred dollars worth of valuable material was destroyed.

The accidents continued. The head came off of a sledge hammer while a man was swinging, hit another man in the crew, and broke his skull. At the rock quarry, a huge boulder broke loose, landed on a man, and crushed his leg. Swarms of wasps came one morning and attacked dozens of men, stinging like mad.

Work slowed. Men refused to follow orders. But

replacement workers had vanished, and Strauser needed every strong back he could get. Every day, Mr. Hoffer brought an angry telegram. The most recent said, "If you cannot get results, I will find a man who can".

Strauser knew it was saboteurs, probably the union organizers or the men he had fired. He watched Santini closely for several days but could never tie him to any accident. He needed to take action.

The saboteurs must be working at night, he thought. There were too many people around during the day for them to not get caught. Strauser would prepare a little surprise for them.

He summoned Santini. He disliked working with the man, but the workers would follow no one else. He told Santini that he needed a couple of strong men for a special job that night and that it would pay five dollars apiece. He told Santini to find the men and meet him at the superintendent's shed at 11:00 PM.

The three men arrived on time, Santini among them. Strauser gave them no greeting but directed them to get picks out of the tool wagon and then to follow him. He carried an unlit lantern. The men noticed that he wore a holster and carried two pistols.

The moon was full that night. Clouds obscured its light now and then, but the group was able to see well enough. They walked along the trolley tracks, Strauser leading them southward in the direction of the Devil's Den, toward where they had found the grave. No one spoke. Before long, they arrived at the rock quarry and halted.

Strauser thought he saw something. He strained his eyes, searching the gloom. It was indistinct at first, so he and the workmen crept quietly forward, edging closer. He could see more clearly now. It was a man. No, wait, there were two men!

The strangers were twenty yards away. Strauser wondered what they were up to, for they seemed to just stand there, hardly moving. One thing he was sure of was that they were up to no good. He struck a match and lit the lantern. He pulled a pistol from his holster and pointed it at the two men. "Don't make a move," he ordered, "I have a gun, and I will use it!"

The strangers remained motionless as if they had not heard him. The glow of the lantern illuminated the nearby rocks and trees, but its light seemed not to touch the two men.

"Who are you? What are you doing here?" Strauser demanded. The two figures turned, faced Strauser and his men, and then stood still. Strauser felt uncertain, for these men were not acting as he expected. "If you do not identify yourselves at once," he threatened, "I will open fire."

Strauser pointed the pistol, and his finger squeezed the trigger. Before he could fire, he heard Santini's voice. "They are behind us!" Santini warned. Strauser spun around. There on the tracks, he saw two more men. Strauser turned the pistol in this new direction. "Up there, there's another one!" a worker yelled, pointing to the right through the trees. "And another!"

Strauser and his men were surrounded. The six strangers encircled them. Slowly, very slowly, they came nearer.

Santini stood impassively. The other two men spoke to each other rapidly and nervously in their native tongue. Strauser's heart beat more quickly. "What are they up to?" he thought. They carried no weapons that Strauser could see, but they seemed hostile and menacing.

The figures came closer. They were distinct now. They were dressed in tattered clothes, practically rags. They seemed to glow in the darkness, even when the scattered clouds hid the moon. They wore battered hats and caps, but their faces were invisible.

The lantern went out.

The workers let out a scream and dropped their picks to the ground, looking wildly around. The figure that was behind them stepped away from the tracks, as if he was opening an escape route. The two workers fled through that opening in terror. Strauser and Santini were alone now, alone with the menacing strangers.

Strauser leveled the gun at the nearest one and fired. The

man stopped and just stood there. He seemed unharmed.

"Dammit!" Strauser yelled and took careful aim. He fired another round, then another. He fired every bullet, emptying the gun. The man remained standing.

Strauser felt fear, the most profound fear he ever knew in his life. He stood there, frozen, the empty pistol still pointed at his target. A hand suddenly touched his shoulder, and he screamed, spinning around, swinging the pistol. A large, powerful hand caught his wrist and held him in an iron grip. It was Santini.

The moonlight illuminated Santini's face. Santini looked unusually calm, and he even smiled. He spoke. "I believe, Mr. Strauser, that you may have encountered these men before. I think they have some business to conduct with you. So I will leave you with your friends". He let go of Strauser, turned, and started to walk in the direction of camp. The figures opened a gap in their ring, allowing him to pass unmolested.

Strauser stood there for several moments, rooted to the ground. The circle of men slowly closed around him. Finally, his rising fear pushed him into action. He tried to flee, running at the figure that blocked the tracks, hoping to knock the man down and escape. He lowered his shoulder, braced for the impact, and smashed into the man.

He hit nothing. He tripped, landing on the stones of the

trolley bed, scraping his hands painfully. He struggled back to his feet, then stopped, screaming in agony. His shoulder felt on fire as if stabbed by daggers of flame. The excruciating pain spread through his entire body. He threw himself to the ground, his howls splitting the night. He felt paralyzed and couldn't breathe.

Suddenly, the pain diminished. His head swam, and he gasped for breath. He got clumsily to his feet, his vision clearing. He was surrounded - the mysterious men were not five yards away.

He pulled out his second pistol and blazed away at point-blank range. Once more, there was no effect.

He saw a gap between two of the men and sprang for it. In an instant, he was past them. He ran through the darkness, tripping over rocks and smashing into trees. He glanced over his shoulder and saw they were pursuing.

The blessed moon reappeared, giving him some light. He saw a stone wall ahead of him and leaped over it. He ran across the field and up the slope, his pursuers on his heels. He fled southeast across the field through the scrub and brush. He reached the top of the ridge, the top of the Devil's Den, running madly across the giant boulders. He did not see the cliff.

He plummeted into the valley below, falling twenty feet to the ground. All was blackness. After a time he awoke. Slowly and painfully, he forced himself to consciousness. He felt horrifying pain in his legs. He could not move them. Blood flowed from his forehead into his eyes, blinding him. He feebly lifted his arm and wiped the blood away with his sleeve. He raised his head and saw a man's legs. He screamed.

He felt his body being lifted, strong hands grabbing him by his arms and his broken legs. They carried him, each step causing him agony, as they jostled and transported him through the night. After what seemed like an eternity, his captors suddenly dropped him to the ground. He lay motionless. He heard something, a sound like digging.

Time passed, but he did not know if it was hours or minutes. The digging noise stopped, and strong hands gripped him again, rolling him onto his back. He glimpsed the full moon as he felt himself being lifted. Suddenly, he was falling again. But not far.

He landed on his back, onto soft ground. He had fallen perhaps fifteen feet. He was in a deep hole, wedged between two huge buried rocks. He could not move his arms. Above him, he saw a square opening. He could see clouds illuminated by the moonlight. He heard a grinding noise and saw something appear at the edge of the opening. It was round and huge. It was a boulder. Someone was pushing it into the hole.

The sound of the huge rock crashing into the hole drowned out Strauser's scream of terror. Sharp fragments of stone lacerated his face, but somehow, he was not crushed. The two rocks that wedged him into his tomb kept the boulder from crushing him.

The boulder rested two feet above his face. Moonlight filtered through the narrow cracks between the boulder and the rocks, just enough light to enable Strauser to see. He was trapped. A minute later there was another crash. A second boulder landed on top of the first.

He heard the digging sound again, and something landed in his eyes. It was dirt. Someone was filling the hole with dirt! He shook his head, frantically blinking his eyes. The dirt soon filled the cracks between the boulder and the rocks, and Strauser now lay in total darkness. With all the ebbing strength he could muster, he cried for help, but no living man heard his screams.

When Strauser failed to show up for work the next day, Mr. Hoffer ordered a search. The workers were given two hours at noontime and were instructed to examine the area where Strauser was last seen. They found nothing. The men were ordered to return to their camp. They made their way back, following the right-of-way of the trolley. Santini was the last man in the slow-moving column.

As he walked past the stone quarry, Santini noticed something unusual. Several large rocks were arranged in an unusual pattern. He went over to the rocks and looked more closely. The soil had recently been disturbed. He saw something very curious, a piece of wood, like a board torn from a crate. One end of the board was stuck into the ground, and near the top of the wood, there was writing. He got down on his knees and examined it closely. Somebody had crudely scribbled something in pencil on the wood, a single word. "Strauser".

He grabbed the narrow board and pulled it out of the ground. "This will make good firewood," he said to no one in particular. He turned away and followed his co-workers back to camp.

Eventually, the trolley line was completed. It became very successful. Each day of the busy summer season, the trolleys carried hundreds of visitors smoothly across the battlefield. One local entrepreneur built a photo studio just south of the Devil's Den, which soon became a popular gathering spot for the local people. For many visitors, it became quite a fad to have their pictures taken while standing on the enormous boulders of the Devil's Den.

A few years after the trolley opened, Conlon's old regiment held a reunion at Gettysburg to celebrate the anniversary of their mustering out of the Union Army. They planned quite a party. The organizers decided to make it a three-day affair and would even camp on the battlefield, despite the fact they were all in their fifties by now. For their campsite, they chose the valley between Little Round Top and the Devil's Den.

They rented the pavilion at the picnic ground near the photo studio and had a celebration on the final evening of their reunion. They brought in huge quantities of delicious food and hired an excellent band. Kegs of beer and cases of whiskey rounded out the feast. The men had a grand time, telling stories, swapping lies, and singing loudly in off-key voices.

Around midnight, Conlon felt a bit light-headed. He decided to take a little walk to sober himself up a bit. The moon was bright that night and the air was cool, perfect conditions for a stroll.

He followed the trolley tracks back toward town. As he strolled, he inhaled the clean night air. The noise of the celebration faded behind him as he walked. It felt good to get away from the cigar smoke.

The tracks made a sharp curve to the right, toward Gettysburg. Conlon followed them for a couple hundred yards. He decided to sit and rest for a few minutes before getting back to the party. He saw a place where several large rocks lay near the tracks. He recognized the old quarry. He sat down on a large stone and stared at the full moon through the gaps in the trees above his head.

It was quiet. He barely heard the noise of the party. He listened to the sound of the insects in the forest. He heard an unusual noise. At first, he thought it might be an owl or the screech of some bird, but the sound did not come from up in the trees. Rather, it came from down low, near the ground. He heard it again, an unpleasant noise, the kind a small mammal might make when it falls victim to the jaws of a carnivore.

The noise seemed close. Conlon stood up and looked around but saw nothing. He heard the noise again, coming from the other side of a round boulder just a few feet away. Curiously, he approached the boulder and peered around it, but there was nothing there. Then he heard the sound again. It seemed to be coming from below him, from under the ground. Perhaps some subterranean animal had been injured and hidden itself in its burrow.

There was something about the sound, something familiar that sparked a long-faded memory.

Conlon decided he had been away from the party long enough. He went back to the tracks and turned south, heading off to rejoin his friends. He walked quickly and did not look back.

You can still see the trolley bed today. It is a pleasant place for a stroll. The tracks are long gone, and the ground has returned much to nature. When you follow it far enough and get away from the cars and buses at the Devil's Den, it is quite peaceful. Sometimes, you will come across boy scouts hiking the trail to earn merit badges, and occasionally, you will see riders on horseback making their way around the battlefield.

Find yourself a nice rock. Take a look around and listen to the sounds of nature. It is hard to believe that the silence of this spot was once shattered by the voices of men in the throes of death. Sometimes, if you listen carefully, you can almost imagine that you hear the voices.

Eddy – An Introduction

The Gettysburg National Military Park is fortunate. There are many people who love the battlefield, people who have enormous respect for the thousands of soldiers who died here, and people who want the battlefield to be well-preserved and well-maintained as a way of honoring the sacrifice those soldiers made. Some of these people volunteer to assist the often overworked Park Rangers. These people may donate money, but some donate another precious commodity – their time. The battlefield is huge, covering 6,000 acres. There are 1,300 monuments on the battlefield, many of them works of art, making the battlefield a vast sculpture garden. It is difficult to protect such a vast outdoor museum. Some people volunteer to drive around the park at night, looking for trouble-makers or vandals and notifying the law-enforcement rangers if something troubling is spotted.

Sometimes, they are sickened by what they see. At times, they find monuments defiled by graffiti. Sometimes, they find holes in the ground dug by someone trying to find relics. Occasionally, they discover destruction, monuments with missing features, or marks of hammer blows. When this happens, they wonder, "Who could have done this? Why do they do this? What are they thinking? What kind of people are they?"

Eddy could have answered those questions. He was one of

those people.

The Sentinel

Decades passed, and the people finally made peace with the land. Digging and construction came to an end. The Devil's Den became part of a preserve, a national military park. Men and women in uniforms, assisted by volunteers, now protected the Devil's Den from destruction and devastation.

The humans who protected the park could not keep continual vigil. The park is vast in area. There were still people who did not respect the land, those who, for various and incomprehensible reasons, would do it harm. On occasion, they disturbed the Spirit that normally lay dormant in the Devil's Den.

Monuments vandalized
Damages estimated at $50,000; some items also stolen

Two things impressed the people who visited Eddy's mobile home. The first thing was the size of the television in Eddy's tiny living room. The second was the bronze skull of a Union soldier that sat on the table next to the TV.

Eddy bought the television at a shopping mall near Harrisburg. He paid cash for it. Eddy got the head of the Union soldier at the Gettysburg National Military Park. He didn't pay anything for it.

The day Eddy brought his television home and set it up in his living room, he threw a party to celebrate. He spent the last of his money on three cases of beer, called two of his buddies, and invited them over to watch the ball game.

His friends brought potato chips and pizzas. They marveled at how great the game looked on the big TV screen. Unfortunately, their team was less than great - by the time the game was three-fourths over, their team was so far behind it was embarrassing. Eddy and his buddies got bored.

"Let's go somewhere," Eddy said. He and his friends got into his pickup truck and drove around in the dark. They didn't particularly care where they went.

Before long, they found themselves on Business Route 15, heading north. Eddy saw dark objects on the side of the road and recognized them as cannons. They had entered Gettysburg National

Military Park. As they continued north, Eddy noticed several monuments dimly illuminated in the moonlight. "Hey," said Eddy, "I got an idea."

Eddy drove around some more as if looking for something. His buddies asked him where they were going, but he wouldn't say. Before long, he pulled off the road and parked in a secluded area. There was no traffic, nor were there lights of any kind to dispel the darkness. Trees by the side of the road obscured the moon.

"Follow me," Eddy said, getting out of the car. He grabbed some tools out of the bed of the truck, as well as a couple pieces of metal pipe. "What are we doing? one of his friends asked. "We're the Confederate Army," Eddy replied, "We're gonna' go get us a Yankee!"

They left the road, crossed a large grassy field, and soon arrived at the place Eddy was looking for. The three men stopped in front of a monument, one of many that dot the Gettysburg Battlefield. The monument portrayed a Union soldier standing at attention upon a squared stone. Words carved around the base told of the men killed and wounded in the battle.

"Let's get to work, boys," Eddy ordered. He and his buddies attacked the statue with pieces of pipe and a sledgehammer. Eddy had brought a piece of rope with him. He made a loop at the end of it and tossed it over the head of the statue. Eddy pulled on the rope while his buddies pried the statue with the pipes and whacked at its foundation with the hammer. After a few strenuous minutes, they finished their work. The statue that had stood on the battlefield for over a century now lay on the soft ground, the soldier's face buried in soft dirt.

Eddy had brought three beers. He and his friends toasted their victory over the monument and tossed the empty cans on the ground. "We better get out of here," one of Eddy's friends suggested, "before somebody comes by." Eddy agreed but said he wanted a souvenir first. He took the hammer, stood over the fallen statue, and brought the hammer down on the neck of the Union soldier. The ancient material gave way easily. The neck broke cleanly as if cut off by a sword. Eddy picked up the severed head, and he and his friends returned to the truck.

Back at the trailer, Eddy proudly set his new possession on the table next to the TV. He and his friends spent the night channel surfing, finishing off the rest of the beer around three in the morning.

The next day, Eddy had a major hangover. For breakfast, he had a cup of black coffee and a slice of pizza from last night. As he consumed his meal, he admired the head of the Union soldier. He felt it made a fine addition to his decor.

Next weekend, Eddy and his pals decided to repeat their outing. This time, they sneaked into the Evergreen Cemetery and knocked over a few tombstones. The following week, they brought cans of spray paint and visited one of the large state monuments on the battlefield. Eddy sprayed the words "Jeff Davis Rules" on the flat stone, laughing at his own cleverness.

After this last visit, Eddy and his friends grew bored with their vandalism. Besides, their team was on a major winning streak, so their weekend nights were usually spent in front of Eddy's huge TV. The people who ran the park at Gettysburg were hopeful that the recent spell of vandalism had ended.

A few months later, when the warmer weather arrived, Eddy and his friends took a trip to the ocean. They loaded the truck with cases of beer and drove down to Ocean City, Maryland. They rented a rundown apartment and spent several days drinking beer and working on their tans.

On the third day, Eddy awoke with his usual hangover. He went out on the balcony to clear his head. He sat down on a cheap lawn chair, breathed in the salt air, and sipped on a warm beer. For a long time, he gazed mindlessly at the waves crashing onto the beach. Then something caught his eye.

He saw an old man walking along the beach just above the high tide line. The man carried some kind of object, a pole about four feet long. Something resembling a large dinner plate was attached to the end of the pole. The man wore headphones, and as he walked, he swung the dinner plate back and forth just inches above the sand. Every now and then, the man would stop scoop up some sand with what looked like a can made out of wire. Sometimes, he would reach into the can, pick something out, and put it in his pocket.

Eddy's curiosity was aroused. He chugged his beer, went down to the beach, and caught up to the old man.

"What are you up to, Pops?" he greeted the man. The old fellow turned around, saw Eddy, smiled, and said hello. "What's that gadget you got there?" Eddy asked, pointing at the dinner plate on a pole.

"Oh, this," the old man replied, "this is my metal detector."

"Metal detector?" Eddy responded, "How does it work?"

"Well, I guess it's a kind of radar or maybe a mine detector. I move the flat, round part back and forth across the sand. If it goes over something made of metal, it starts beeping. Then I dig it up to see what it is. Take a look at what I found just this morning."

The man reached into his deep pocket and pulled out a handful of small objects. Eddy looked at what the man held in his hand. There were a lot of coins, mostly pennies, several keys, and a cheap-looking watch with a metal band.

"I find lots of good stuff," said the old man enthusiastically.

"Just last week, I found a coin purse someone lost. Besides the coins, there were seventy dollars in it."

Eddy had always loved gadgets. He especially couldn't resist a gadget that offered the prospect of money that he didn't have to work for. He asked the old man where he bought his metal detector. One hour later, Eddy was at that store. Fortunately, he had just made the minimum payment on his credit card and could charge his purchase. Eddy spent the rest of the day walking the beach with his new toy.

By the next morning, he was bored with it. That afternoon, he and his buddies returned home. Eddy stuck the metal detector in his junk-filled closet and went back to watching his large-screen TV.

A couple weeks later, Eddy and a friend were in the town of Gettysburg, waiting for happy hour to begin at a local tavern. They wandered the streets to kill time. Eddy looked through the window of a store that displayed a sign proclaiming "Civil War Memorabilia." There were several small objects lying in a velvet-lined case. A sign next to the case identified the items - "Uniform Button", ".58 Caliber Musket Ball," and "Belt Buckle". He was incredulous at the prices asked for the objects.

"Who in their right mind would pay that much money for pieces of junk?" Eddy asked his buddy. "There are lots of people who collect crap like that," the man replied, "Civil War nuts."

"Where does this garbage come from?" Eddy asked. "Probably someone digs it up," his buddy answered, "and sells it to stores like this. Hell, there's probably tons of it still buried here around Gettysburg".

Eddy looked again at the price tags in the store window and remembered his metal detector. "You mean a guy like me can just go out in a field somewhere, dig this stuff up, and sell it for good money?" "Sure," his buddy answered, "except it's illegal."

That statement got Eddy's interest. He was between jobs, a condition he often found himself in, and he was looking for some easy money. Eddy was a strange guy. You could make him an offer - earn ten dollars in exchange for one hour of honest labor or make one buck for ten hours of dishonest work. Given the choice, Eddy would always choose the latter.

During happy hour, as he drank his half-priced beers, Eddy made his plans. He went to work that very night.

He had a buddy drop him off on the battlefield around midnight. He was afraid to leave his own truck parked anywhere, thinking the police would find that suspicious. The buddy would pick him up in two hours. In exchange for this service, Eddy paid one six-pack of premium beer.

He brought his metal detector with him, as well as a small shovel, a plastic grocery bag, and a cold twelve-pack. He soon found a secluded spot and got to work. He found a couple of things that he hoped might have some value, a small hunk of metal and two round objects. He left behind seven empty beer cans, two candy bar wrappers, and a sizable hole in the soft ground.

He visited the battlefield a few more times over the following weeks. Sometimes, he found things, but usually he didn't. He knew a man in town who would buy his illegal stuff. The amount of money he earned certainly didn't justify the amount of labor he expended, but for some reason, Eddy enjoyed his work.

In the mornings, park rangers or tourists would come across Eddy's handiwork. The overloaded maintenance crew would come out, pick up the litter, and try to repair the damage. The rangers stepped up their nighttime patrols, but they were few in number, and the park was very large. Eddy's visits went undetected.

One evening, Eddy had his buddy drop him off at the Peach Orchard. He walked east through a moonlit field and came to the trail that follows the old trolley line. He headed south and soon came to his destination - a triangular field bordered by walls of stone.

The field is just west of the Devil's Den and sits on the slope of a hill. It was at this place the fighting began on the second day of the battle. Texas soldiers of General John Bell Hood's division attacked up the slope, and Union soldiers from New York drove them back but were in turn flanked by Rebels from Georgia. By the time the fighting ended, the field was covered with dozens of corpses.

The week before, Eddy actually hired a professional guide for a tour of the battlefield. He wanted to know where the heaviest fighting had been, as he figured that could increase his odds of success if he dug where the most shooting occurred. Not only was the triangular field a scene of heavy fighting, but it also was away from the usual tourist paths. Eddy figured he could work unseen by rangers who would be patrolling the park roads.

Eddy went to work along the west edge of the field, not far from the stone wall. His first two diggings turned up nothing, but the third was a different story.

Eddy's shovel hit something hard a foot underground. At first, he thought it was a tree root or a buried stone. He cleared the dirt from the top of the object with his fingers, feeling that it was round and smooth. He hoped maybe it was a cannon ball. He dug around it and was soon able to pry it out of the soil. He held it up in the pale light and whistled softly. It was a skull, a human skull.

Eddy pondered the object for a few seconds, wondering if it was worth any money. He went back to work with his shovel and soon unearthed a bunch of bones, human bones. They undoubtedly belonged to the same man whose skull Eddy had exhumed. As he dug the bones out of the ground, he loaded them into a plastic garbage bag. Before long, he unearthed a quarter of a human skeleton.

Eddy took a seat on the stone wall and served himself another beer as a reward for his labors. He looked at his watch - it was time to head back to his rendezvous. He threw his empty beer can into the hole he had made, picked up the metal detector and the bag of bones, and headed back along the old trolley trail.

The next day, he told his connection in town about what he had found. The man told Eddy that his find was worthless - nobody would buy a human skeleton, not even the most unscrupulous collectors. Disappointed, Eddy returned to his mobile home.

He pulled the skull out of the garbage bag and stared at it for a moment like Hamlet pondering Yorick. Then he had an inspiration. He put the skull on the table next to the head of the Union soldier. He tossed the bag of bones behind the sofa on top of a pile of dirty clothes. He rummaged in his closet until he found an old baseball cap. The logo said "Yankees." He placed the cap on the skull and laughed uproariously at his own joke. "Welcome to your new home, soldier boy!" Eddy said to the skull, "I trust you will find your new accommodations to be satisfactory. Beats the heck out of bein' covered with dirt. I will now leave you and your new Yankee friend to swap war stories." With that, he went out to buy cigarettes. That night, he had his buddies over to admire his new conversation piece.

Eddy made another trip to the battlefield the following week, deciding to return to the triangular field. As before, his buddy dropped him off by the Peach Orchard a little before midnight. Eddy again made his way across the field and down the old trolley trail. The moon was full and the sky cloudless, so Eddy had no trouble finding his way.

He went to work in the northwest corner of the field. Before long, half a dozen shallow holes had scarred the surface of the field. Half a dozen beer cans lay on the grass. Eddy was getting tired and had found nothing of value. He stopped to rest. The night was warm, and he was hot and sweaty. Eddy wiped his forehead with the back of his hand, caught his breath, and went back to work. Suddenly, he heard a noise.

Something had flown past his head, going at a great rate of speed. It had passed about three feet from him, and it made a loud buzzing noise. "Bug," thought Eddy, "big one," guessing it was a large bee. Eddy didn't know that bees don't fly at night.

Eddy popped open another beer and gulped a few sips. There was another loud buzzing noise, and something passed through the air just a foot away. Eddy heard a loud splat. "Stupid bug flew right into the stone wall!" thought Eddy. He went to the wall and walked up to a large stone with a white mark on it, right at the spot where he thought he heard the splat. He looked closely, expecting to see the rock covered with smashed bugs. Instead, he saw a small crater in the stone. He felt the inside of it and looked at his finger in the bright moonlight. His fingertip was covered with a fine white powder instead of bug innards.

Eddy's curiosity was aroused. Both times, the bugs seemed to come from the same direction, from the south end of the field. Eddy climbed up on a nearby boulder and peered in that direction. Despite the bright moonlight, he saw nothing. Suddenly, at the edge of the field, he saw a flash of light. A fraction of a second later, another buzzing object flew past his head and smashed into the trees behind him.

"Lightning bug?" Eddy wondered. "That was awfully bright for a lightning bug. Besides, they don't fly that fast."

He stood motionless on the boulder, staring toward the south end of the field, illuminated by the bright moon. Again, he saw a bright flash of light. This time, he did not hear a buzzing noise. Instead, he felt pain, the most agonizing pain he had ever known in his life.

It felt like someone had taken a long railroad spike and heated it in a flame until it glowed red and then driven it through the flesh of his thigh with a sledgehammer. Eddy spun around, fell off the boulder, and crashed to the ground. He lay on his back screaming, oblivious to anything but the pain.

After a minute or so, the pain lessened just a bit. He raised his head and looked at the leg, expecting to see a horrible wound. But his leg looked normal.

He felt the thigh with his hand. The hand felt wet as if covered with warm liquid. He held the hand in front of his face, expecting to see it dripping with blood, but the hand looked dry. The skin shone white in the bright moonlight.

He raised himself up with his arms, pushed himself over to a nearby rock, and lay against it. His thigh throbbed with pain. He tried to move his injured leg and successfully wiggled his foot. The leg of his pants felt wet, and the wetness seemed to be spreading from his thigh. He felt his pant leg becoming soaked by a warm liquid. But he could see the leg clearly in the bright moonlight, and it looked normal. Eddy began to feel weak.

Without knowing why, Eddy pulled off the shoe from the foot of his uninjured leg. Frantically, he pulled out the lace. He was wearing heavy work boots, and his laces were strong and thick. He wrapped the lace around his thigh above the spot where he felt the pain. He pulled the lace as tight as he could and knotted it. He pulled a jackknife out of his pocket and placed it on the knot. He tied the loose ends of the lace around the knife and twisted and twisted the knife. The lace grew tighter and tighter, biting into the skin of

Eddy's thigh. When it was as tight as he could make it, Eddy tied the knife into place. He lay his head back against the rock, breathing deeply. In a few minutes, he felt a little better. The pain was subsiding into a dull throb, and he felt less light-headed.

Eddy had no idea what had happened to him, but he knew one thing for certain. He wanted to get away from the triangular field.

He pulled himself over to a larger boulder and hoisted himself to his feet. When he put weight on the injured leg, a sharp pain shot through the thigh, but Eddy clenched his teeth and hung on until the pain began to subside. He tried to take a step and found he was able to limp slowly and painfully.

He looked around for his metal detector and saw it on the grass ten feet away. He limped over to it, supporting himself against another boulder, and reached to pick it up. There was another buzzing sound, and something struck one of the full beer cans that lay on the ground next to the metal detector. The can exploded, showering Eddy with beer.

Eddy decided he no longer cared about the metal detector or the unopened beer. The only thing he cared about was getting away from the triangular field as fast as he could.

Eddy limped as quickly as his throbbing leg allowed. The west edge of the field was only a few yards away. He reached the stone wall that marked the border of the field. The wall was not very high, but Eddy had difficulty climbing it because of his injured leg. Above his head, Eddy noticed a tree branch hanging over the wall. He grabbed it and used it to pull himself to the top of the wall. His foot slipped on the round stones, and he struggled to keep his balance. For a second, he stood atop the wall, illuminated by the bright moon. From the corner of his eye, he saw a bright flash from the south edge of the field. An instant later, something smashed into his shoulder with enormous force.

He was knocked off the wall and landed painfully on the tree's exposed roots. His arm throbbed with horrible pain just below the shoulder. He tried to move the arm but couldn't. It lay limp at his side. But he could see the arm, and it looked normal.

Eddy could do nothing but lie on his back on the forest floor, enduring waves of pain from his injured limbs. He was scared, more scared than he had ever been in his life. He wanted to get up and flee, to run away from the triangular field and get back to his mobile home and his television, but he could not move.

For several minutes, he lay there, feeling nothing but pain and fear. But then he heard a noise that turned his fear into terror.

Eddy heard something moving. The noise was coming from the south. He could hear twigs snapping and tree branches rustling. It sounded like the noises made by a person walking in the woods.

The noises were coming closer.

The moon was still rising in the east. Its light illuminated the place where Eddy lay. He looked around in horror, wanting only to get up and run away, but he could only lie there as the noises grew louder and louder.

Eddy thought he saw something moving about twenty yards away. He heard the sound of another twig snap, this time fifteen yards away. He screamed in terror, his eyes frantically searching for the source of the sound.

He heard another noise, but this time, it was not the sound of someone walking. He heard a loud click. It sounded metallic and came from just five yards away. Suddenly, Eddy saw a bright flash of light. It was the last thing he saw.

The following day was sunny and cool, with a steady breeze blowing from the west. It was a perfect day for hiking. By noon, the trails of Gettysburg National Military Park were filled with hikers, tourists, and local residents out for a stroll.

The old trolley path was a favorite of many hikers. There was a parking lot by the Devil's Den not twenty yards from the trail. From the Den, the trail goes west for a short distance, then turns sharply north. The trail runs straight as an arrow for several hundred yards. If you walk the path in that direction and look to your right, you can see a stone wall, and beyond it, there is a hill sloping up to the ridge above the Devil's Den.

A group of Scouts came up the trail, a dozen boys and two troop leaders. Several boys had walking sticks that they used as pretend rifles, shooting at imaginary enemies in the distant trees.

One boy did not have a stick. He was envious of his fellow scouts and felt he was missing out on the fun. His eyes searched for a suitable stick but found nothing.

The two scout leaders stopped, and one pulled out a map to determine their location. The boy decided to take advantage of this pause in the hike. He left the path heading to his right, hoping to find a suitable stick near the stone wall.

He saw a solitary tree. It looked like a big limb had recently fallen from the tree. He ran over to the tree and looked around. Soon, he spotted a perfect stick lying next to the stone wall. Then he spotted something else. A body!

He screamed and ran back to the trail as fast as he could, stumbling over rocks and underbrush. He rushed to the bewildered scout leaders, screaming to them, trying to tell them what he had seen. In a minute, they calmed the boy, and he told them of his discovery. The two men followed the boy back through the trees to the stone wall. Soon they, too saw it - the body of a young man, lying on the ground, not moving.

One of the leaders pulled out his phone dialed 911, and told the dispatcher to send help. The other man went up to the body, looking for signs of life. He put his ear to its chest and listened for breathing, but he heard none. He felt the wrist for a pulse, but there was nothing.

The man with the phone went back to the trail and gathered up the rest of the boys. The other man stayed near the body. Soon, a park ranger arrived in a jeep. A few minutes later, another vehicle arrived with two more men, one of whom was a paramedic. The scout leader's diagnosis was soon confirmed. The young man had been dead for several hours.

They placed the body on a stretcher and carried it to the Jeep. They drove carefully up the trail to the nearest park road, where an ambulance was waiting. They loaded the body into the vehicle, and it was taken to the Adams County morgue.

The park rangers and two policemen inspected the area near the body. They soon found the holes in the earth that Eddy had dug, as well as the metal detector and several empty beer cans. Eddy's prized possessions were soon on their way to the police station.

A look through Eddy's wallet revealed his identity and a detective was dispatched to his mobile home. The detective found no clues that would help solve the mystery of Eddy's death, but he did find the skull and the bag of bones, which he sent to a laboratory for analysis.

The county coroner soon arrived at the morgue and began his autopsy. He read the police report for clues as to the cause of Eddy's death. He first looked for skull injuries, thinking Eddy had fallen and hit his head on a rock. He found a few scrapes and scratches but no evidence of any serious head injury. He checked in vain for bullet holes or stab wounds. Eddy's blood alcohol level was elevated but not to a life-threatening degree, and there was no evidence of any drug use.

After several hours of meticulous, exacting work, the coroner called it quits. He poured himself a cup of coffee and went to his desk to fill out his paperwork. On one of the forms, there was a large empty block. The words at the top of the block said "Cause of Death." The coroner wrote a single word in the empty space - "Unknown."

Three days later, Eddy was buried. Few people attended the funeral. The skull and bones of the Confederate soldier were buried, too. Experts from the Park identified the button that Eddy had thrown in with the bones and concluded that the man had been a Texan. The Rebel soldier's remains were carefully packed and sent to Texas to be buried alongside other men of that state who had fallen in the Civil War.

It seemed to the Park Rangers that incidences of vandalism

decreased in the following weeks, but they did not stop completely. The amount of damage done to the park dropped a bit, but damage still occurred. There were other people like Eddy around. The park rangers tried to catch the Eddy's and put a stop to their work. But the Gettysburg National Battlefield Park is a very big place, and the Rangers are few in number. The Park is vulnerable to people like Eddy.

It is too bad the National Park Service cannot afford more guards to watch over the battlefield, guards who would patrol the fields and forests at night to defend it against its enemies, against people like Eddy.

In July of 1863, there were plenty of guards at Gettysburg. For three days, the armies of North and South fought. At night, after the shooting stopped, the survivors would try to settle down for a few pitiful hours of rest before taking up arms again the following day. But for many of the men, there was no rest.

The two armies camped for the night just a few hundred yards apart. Both sides feared danger in the night. Both were wary of spies from the enemy side, spies who might ferret out the next day's battle plans or harm sleeping men.

Officers would go among the weary men and select the unlucky ones to be guards during the night. The men would grab a quick meal, if they had any food, and go off to their work. These men would grumble and rail against the unfairness of what they were being told to do, but they would follow their orders. They would pick up their rifles and deploy around their camp.

Each sentry would go to his post and settle in for his stint of duty. He would seek a place where he could look out over the landscape, a place where he could see but not be seen. Perhaps he would take position behind a tree at the edge of a woods or perhaps behind a wall or a fence at the edge of a field.

The sentry would pick his spot and make himself as comfortable as he could. His rifle would be loaded, and his cartridge box filled with ammunition. He would stare out into the darkness, watching. During the Battle of Gettysburg, a full moon aided him in his work.

For hours, the sentinel would sit, fighting off sleep. He would think about his duty to his comrades and how they depended upon him for protection. There would be nothing to relieve his boredom - unless he saw someone.

At the first hint of something moving in the distance, the sentry would snap to attention. He would raise his rifle to his shoulder and rivet his eyes on the trespasser. But he had to be careful, for the vague figure could just as easily befriend as foe. Perhaps the sentry saw an enemy spy, or perhaps he saw a comrade that had gotten lost. The sentry would watch and listen, anxious for a sign that would tell him if this trespasser was a friend or enemy.

Occasionally, the distant figure would betray its intentions. It would do something that looked threatening or that posed a danger to the sentry's comrades. If that happened, the sentry would act. He would steady his rifle on a fence rail or a rock or a tree, carefully gauge the distance to his target, and center it in his gun sights. He would wait for his enemy to stop to make himself a better target. He would hold his breath and squeeze his trigger. Bright flame would flash from the barrel of his gun, and his bullet would speed through the air to reach his target.

The Gettysburg battlefield is a quiet place today. The thunder of cannon and crackle of muskets has long disappeared. The nights are no longer illuminated by the campfires of exhausted men. Keen-eyed sentries no longer peer out across every field. There are no more guardians who strike down their enemies at night. At least, not that anyone knows of.

Jason and Lucas – An Introduction

As a Licensed Battlefield Guide, Helen had done many bus tours. Because it was May, all three tours had been school groups on their way to or from Washington DC, stopping at Gettysburg for the "history" part of their field trip. Helen never imagined that the three worst tours of her career would occur in one day. It was almost always possible to find a way to get kids interested. Today was the exception.

When she got on her first bus, she was told that they had driven from Indiana, starting at 7:00 PM the day before and that the kids would get breakfast after the tour. At her second bus, the teacher in charge gave her a list of nine specific battlefield locations to visit, told her to let the kids climb one observation tower and the Pennsylvania Monument, allow time for taking pictures, and to be done in 45 minutes, not the scheduled two hours. On her third tour, as she pointed at and explained the statues at the North Carolina Monument, she heard yelling and, to her horror, saw two students fighting, and one had a knife! To her relief, as she dialed 911, other students separated the fighting ones, and a teacher confiscated the knife.

As she walked to her car, she encountered her fellow guide, Jack, who asked her how her day had gone. She described her day. He said to her, "That's why I only do car tours," and walked toward the visitor center.

Helen could not help feeling a little annoyed. Jack was a good guide and loved the battlefield as much as she did. But Helen knew that the much older Jack was retired and had a pension. Bus tours paid better. She needed the money.

Santayana

The Devil's Den has existed for millions of years. Time means nothing to the boulders. The Spirit that inhabits the Den cares little about time. To that power, yesterday and tomorrow are the same. But the horrible things that occurred at the Devil's Den harmed time itself. The power of the Spirit of the Devil's Den disturbed the flow of time, creating eddies and whirlpools in the years that passed over it. Yesterday could become today, and today could become last year.

Could anything be more boring than this?" Jason thought. "Probably not."

He was here because he got a "D" in history last quarter. When his parents heard that Jason's history teacher was offering extra credit to any student who went on the field trip to Gettysburg, they forced him to go. That was why he was wasting a Saturday at the Gettysburg National Military Park.

He had to be at the school at 7:00 AM to meet the bus. Everyone else going on the trip was a history nerd, so there was no one to talk to. And it took two hours to get there.

The first thing they did when they arrived was hiring some guy to give them a tour - that was as exciting as watching "Sixty Minutes." They drove around for hours looking at rocks and trees - really exciting stuff. Every few minutes the guide would stop the bus and make everyone get out. Then he'd point at statues and old fences and fields full of cows and ramble on about something or other. "Over there was where a lot of guys shot a bunch of other guys. And at that place, some more guys got shot by a mess of other guys." Oh, it was so fascinating.

Finally, it was lunchtime. They had a whole hour to do whatever they wanted. But did they stop at Burger King or McDonald's? Of course not! Instead, everybody had to bring a brown bag so as not to waste time.

Jason sat on a large rock, slowly eating his sandwich. One thing was sure, this place had a lot of rocks. Big ones. That had to be the reason they chose this place for their lunch break - you got to look at big rocks while you ate your lunch!

He watched a couple of the nerds from the history club climbing around on top of the big piles of rocks. "The Devil's Den," somebody called it. Talk about a catchy name! Jason didn't expect that any of the nerds would liven things up by falling and smashing their skulls. He couldn't get that lucky, not today. He looked again at his phone. Forty more minutes to kill before they got back on the bus and went to see more places where a bunch of guys shot another bunch of other guys. It looked like the afternoon would be as exciting as the morning.

Jason figured it was time for a cigarette. He had a pack in his brown bag. It was the only thing in the brown bag that he liked. He figured he'd better find a more hidden place to have his smoke. If Mr. History Teacher saw him, he'd get all bent out of shape, and Jason didn't need any more grief right now.

He went back a little way into the woods and found another rock to sit on. If you like rocks, he thought, this is the place to be! He could still see the tops of the biggest rocks of the Devil's Den, but the trees blocked the view of the parking lot. He pulled out a Marlboro, lit it, and sat down to kill more time. When he was half finished with his cigarette Jason suddenly got a funny feeling. He turned and looked around. He discovered he was not alone.

Some guy stood about ten feet from him, looking at him. He was young, probably a year or so older than Jason, and pretty seedy-looking. His clothes were torn in several places and looked like they needed washing. The guy smiled at Jason. "Can you spare me a cigarette?" he asked.

Jason didn't reply. He wasn't too sure about this guy. But then the stranger reached into a brown paper bag and pulled something out. It was a can of Budweiser. He held it out to Jason. "I'll trade," the stranger offered.

He found Jason's weak spot. A beer sure would be good now, Jason realized. The weather was warm, and nothing helped pass the time like a cold can of brew! Jason hesitated a second, then reached into his pack of cigarettes. He held one out to the stranger. "Deal," Jason told him.

The two made their exchange. Jason examined the beer closely and concluded that it looked all right. The stranger pulled a second beer out of the paper bag, popped it open, and drank. Jason figured it must be safe enough and did the same.

The beer was not ice cold, but it was cold enough. It tasted mighty fine. The stranger sat down ten feet from Jason. The two did not speak, but the stranger would occasionally nod at Jason and smile.

When he was finished, Jason crumpled the beer can and threw it on the ground. The stranger did likewise. He stared off into the distance for a few seconds, then turned to Jason and spoke. "Want another one? I got a few more hidden up the hill a bit".

Jason wasn't sure he should trust the guy, but he seemed harmless enough. He looked at his watch to see how much time he still had to kill and found he had plenty. "Might as well do something to pass the time," he said to himself. "Let's go," he told the stranger.

Jason followed the fellow along a trail through the woods. They soon came to a place where there were some really huge boulders. There were two the size of small houses, with a triangular space between them. The man went over to an old log that lay in the space between the boulders. He picked up a small cooler from behind it, set it on the ground, and sat down on the log. "Help yourself", he invited.

The cooler held four more cans of beer. Jason pulled one out and downed it in five swallows. He got another beer from the cooler and sat down a few feet from the stranger. The beers were starting to hit him, and he felt his mood improving.

The stranger struck up a conversation. "Here on a field trip?" he asked.

"You got it," Jason replied. "You too?"

"Naw, I'm from around here," he answered. "Not originally, but I've been here a long time. Seen a lot of people come here on field trips. Looks pretty dull".

"You got that right," Jason responded. He was starting to think this guy was all right.

The stranger held out his hand. "My name's Lucas," he offered. Jason accepted the hand and shook it. "I'm Jason," he replied.

There was silence for a minute or so. Then Lucas reached into a pocket and pulled something out. Jason could not see what it was until the man held it out to him. It was a wishbone, probably from a chicken.

"Do you believe in wishes?" Lucas asked. "Hell, no!" was Jason's response. Lucas continued to hold out the wishbone. "Go on, make a wish," he insisted.

"What the heck!" Jason answered. It couldn't hurt to amuse the guy. He grabbed the end of the wishbone and looked at Lucas. "I wish something exciting would happen around here," he said. He pulled on the end of the bone and heard a snap.

Instantly, Jason was overwhelmed by a strange sensation. He felt like he was falling. He was surrounded by a brilliant light, and a loud rushing noise filled his ears. As quickly as they started, the sensations ended. Jason shook his head, startled. He looked in his hand and saw half of the wishbone - the winning half. Then Jason realized that everything looked different. A lot different.

He looked at his clothing and saw he was no longer wearing his jeans and T-shirt. His pants were light brown, his shirt a dirty gray, and he wore a backpack. He held a long, heavy object in one hand.

Lucas, too, looked different. He was dressed in clothes identical to Jason's. For several seconds, the two young men stood staring at each other. Suddenly, the woods around them erupted in a great noise. Lucas let out an oath, ran to a nearby tree, and hid behind it.

Jason looked around. He had no idea where he was or what was going on. He was no longer in the triangular place between the huge rocks - he was now on a hillside, surrounded by trees. He was also surrounded by crowds of men and overwhelmed by terrifying noise.

The men were dressed like himself and Lucas. There were dozens of them, maybe hundreds, all yelling and screaming. The air was filled with smoke and smelled like sulfur. The men all had long objects in their hands and were doing frantic things with them. The men shoved sticks into and out of the long objects, put them to their shoulders, and pointed them uphill. Flashes of light and explosions erupted from the objects. They were guns, Jason realized. The men were shooting guns!

He looked down at the object in his hand and realized that he, too, held a gun.

He looked up the hill in the direction the men were shooting but could barely see through the thick smoke. A gap appeared in the smoke, and in the distance, he saw things moving, lots of things. Whatever they were, they were hidden behind rocks and obscured by trees. Suddenly, Jason realized that these moving things were also men.

Jason heard the yell of a man's voice. There was a flash of movement all along the distant line of men, followed by another yell. Suddenly, the line of men disappeared behind a great burst of flame and smoke. Jason saw dozens of flashes of light and heard the sound of many explosions. The air around him was filled with buzzing objects flying at incredible speed. A man to his right screamed, and Jason saw him grab his stomach and fall to the ground.

Jason looked once more up the slope. A man a few feet in front of him pointed his gun at the distant men on the hill. Suddenly, the man pitched directly backward, smashing into Jason and bowling him over. Jason pushed the man off of him. He stared in horror at his shirt sleeve. It was covered with blobs of red and yellow matter.

Jason screamed in terror and tossed his gun to the ground. There was a large tree a few yards behind him. He jumped behind it, putting the trunk between himself and the men who were shooting at him. He lay face down on the ground, frantically trying to bury himself in the dead leaves and soft dirt.

He lay there while the madness of noise and smoke swirled around him. His terror abated a bit during a pause in the bedlam. He debated between staying behind the sheltering tree or running for safety while the firing was stopped. He lifted his head a bit to see what was happening up the hill. Suddenly, he felt a stinging pain on the back of his thighs.

Jason turned frantically around, wondering what had happened to him. He froze. He lay on his back, not moving a muscle. The tip of a sword was two inches from his nose. The long blade was held by an angry-looking, red-bearded man who also held a pistol.

The man stared into Jason's eyes and moved the sword point closer. "You will pick up your gun, and you will get back into the battle," he commanded, "If you do not do so, I will kill you."

Jason cowered. He did not know who the man was, but he knew he was not joking. Jason did not know what to do. He said nothing. He just lay there frozen.

The red-bearded man moved his sword away and pointed a pistol at Jason's forehead. He pulled back the hammer of the weapon and wrapped his finger around the trigger. He spoke one word - "Now!"

The word was enough to spur Jason into action. He rolled onto his hands and knees, using the tree trunk to help him to his feet. He was trapped between two terrors. He decided that the terror of the hidden men up the hill was not as great as the terror of the man with the red beard and pistol. He stumbled up the hill a few yards, leaving the protection of the tree.

He tripped over something, falling face-first into the dirt. He felt for the object that had tripped him - it was the gun he had discarded.

He looked behind him and saw that the red-bearded man was watching him, his pistol pointed menacingly. Jason got back to his feet, picked up his rifle, and pointed it up the hill. He began to yell and scream like the other men around him.

He pulled the trigger. Nothing happened. Jason had no idea what he was supposed to do.

He watched the man next to him. The fellow reached into a pouch on his belt, pulled out a small object, put it to his mouth, and bit it. He put the object to the end of his gun barrel, did something with it, and then pulled a stick out from under his gun. He pushed the stick down the gun barrel, withdrew it, replaced the stick, and brought the gun to his hip. Jason could not see what the man did next, but he saw him put the gun to his shoulder, take aim, and fire.

Jason reached for his side and felt his own pouch. He reached in, feeling a number of cylindrical objects. He pulled one out and held it before his face, puzzled. It was a cylinder made of paper, heavy for its size. He remembered what the man had done, put the cylinder to his lips, and bit off a loose flap of paper. He felt a bitter taste on his tongue and wiped his lips with his hand. The back of his hand was covered with a black powder.

He watched another man to see what he did and followed suit. He poured the powder down the barrel of his rifle. He shoved the heavy bullet into the mouth of the gun. He found the stick slung beneath the gun barrel, pulled it out, and used it to push the bullet down the gun barrel. He withdrew the stick and threw it on the ground. He raised the gun to his shoulder, pointed it up the hill, and pulled the trigger. Nothing happened.

Jason heard a musical sound - the sound of a trumpet. Behind him, men started yelling, "Fall back, fall back." The men around him began moving slowly back down the hill, stopping to fire their weapons as they went. Jason turned downhill and went with them. He glanced back over his shoulder as he made his way downhill, looking nervously toward the dark shapes on the hill's upper slope.

He bumped into something and turned to see what it was. He came face-to-face with the red-bearded man. The fellow grabbed him by the throat, almost lifting him off the ground. "I'll be watching you!" he roared, "be sure you stop with the rest of the regiment." He released Jason and went off through the trees, yelling orders and waving his sword above his head.

Jason could see the gray-clad men assembling further to the rear and joined up with a group of them. One of the figures looked familiar. It was Lucas! Jason ran up to him and grabbed onto the front of Lucas' shirt. "Where are we?" Jason demanded, "What's going on?"

Lucas looked at him and laughed. "You wanted excitement," he said. "Welcome to Little Round Top!"

Jason had no idea what Lucas meant. Before he could ask a question, he heard the sound of men yelling. "Form up, form up, get into line!" men screamed. One of the men doing the screaming was red beard. Jason had no idea what was happening. Lucas grabbed his shoulder and spoke. "Stay by me," he told Jason, "and do what I do." Jason obeyed.

Dozens of men formed into a long line, elbow touching elbow. Jason and Lucas were in the middle of the line. The men pointed the barrels of their guns up the hill and started walking back up the slope. "Come on!" Lucas yelled, pulling Jason along, "You'll miss the fun."

The line of men marched steadily up the slope. From the hillside above them, they saw the flash of rifles and heard the thunder of explosions. The air was alive with buzzing sounds, and here and there, men fell to the ground, screaming in agony.

The line of men stopped, feverishly loaded their rifles, and shot back at the men further up the slope. Jason tried again and again to fire his gun, never with success.

The firing from the men above them stopped. Jason watched to see what was happening. He saw movement among the men above him, saw the glint of light upon metal. He heard a powerful voice call out a command. "Bayonets!" the voice yelled, "Right wheel! Charge!" He saw dark shapes of men approaching, running down the hill directly at him. He stood transfixed as the shapes came nearer and nearer.

Ten feet in front of him, a gray-clad man worked feverishly to load his weapon as the line of dark-colored men charged closer and closer. The gray-clad man finished loading and raised the gun to his shoulder. Before he could fire, a man from the approaching line lunged at him, stabbing him with a long object. Jason watched in horror as the gray-clad man was impaled. Jason saw the man double over, six inches of reddened steel appearing through the back of the man's shirt.

Jason dropped his gun and fled. He tripped over tree roots and stumbled over rocks but stayed on his feet. Jason was not alone in his flight. Most of the gray-clad men were also running, fleeing from the advancing line of men. Jason glimpsed the red-bearded man firing his pistol at the approaching figures, then suddenly spun around and fell to the ground.

Jason ran as fast as he could. Some of the men around him dropped their guns to the ground and raised their hands above their heads. Jason dodged them, weaving between the trees, trying to keep ahead of the pursuing line of dark-colored men.

He was running uphill now. He glanced over his shoulder and saw that the line of dark-colored men had slowed, that the gap between him and them was increasing. He redoubled his efforts, leaping over fallen trees and rocks. He tripped over a tree root and crashed to the ground. He felt a hand grab his shoulder, pulling him to his feet. The hand belonged to Lucas. "Better keep moving, friend," he told Jason, "unless you like prisoner-of-war camps."

The two continued their flight. The sound of rifle fire had lessened, but a new and more terrifying sound now filled the air - cannon fire! Artillery shells tore through the trees above their heads, exploding above them in a shower of hot metal. A shell exploded ten feet from them. Both men were blown through the air by the explosion and landed heavily on the forest floor. Neither could move. Both passed into darkness.

Jason awoke. It was dark. His right arm pained him horribly. He looked around to see where he was. Dozens of men lay on the ground all around him, many of them moaning and screaming in pain. He saw that they were in a small clearing in the woods. A fire burned brightly in the middle of the group of men, and moonlight cast a glow over the eerie scene.

Jason saw a large, dirty bandage on his aching arm. It was red with dried blood. Jason felt a terrible thirst. Between moans of pain, he called out for water. A man with a bucket heard him and approached. He dipped a ladle into the bucket and held it to Jason's lips. It was water, blessed water.

Jason grabbed the man's free hand. "Where am I?" he asked, "what happened?"

"This is the field hospital of Hood's Division, Longstreet's Corp, Army of Northern Virginia," the man told him, "although General Hood ain't up to doing much commanding, seeing as he's a patient here himself. Looks like you got a piece of a Yankee shell in your arm, but it ain't that bad. The surgeons didn't cut the arm off, so they must figure you'll be all right." The man then continued on his rounds.

After a while, Jason felt a bit stronger. He became sore from lying down. He got slowly and painfully to his feet. The world spun around him for a minute, but soon, the dizzy feeling passed. He wandered around the moonlit clearing in a daze.

On the far side of the same clearing, Lucas awoke, too. Like Jason, he was in pain, but a different kind of pain, a mind-rending pain that burned like fire and throbbed without pause. Lucas looked down at the place where the pain came from. The bright campfire cast a yellow glow upon him, and Lucas realized his body did not look right. There was a piece of it missing. Jason saw rope-like structures sticking out of a gaping hole in the side of his body.

He screamed. He, too, felt a horrible thirst and cried out for someone to help him. A tall, thin, bearded man approached him. In his hand, the man held a book. He knelt next to Lucas, put a hand on his shoulder, and spoke to him between the young man's cries of pain.

"Your wound is mortal, son," the man said to him. "The doctors say you will live but a few hours."

The man's words penetrated the fog in Lucas' mind. He felt terror. "No!" he screamed, "please, no!"

The man gripped his shoulder with a strong, bony hand. He held the book out to Lucas. "You can find comfort in the Lord," the man said to him. "Let me read to you from the good book." He opened the bible and began to read aloud, but Lucas could not focus on the words or their meaning. He could only recognize the horrible pain that filled his body. He lay there moaning as the man read on and on.

While Lucas received these ministrations, Jason roamed aimlessly around the clearing, looking at the faces of the various wounded men. He was looking for something, but he did not know what it was. He came upon a pair of men, one of whom was standing and reciting from a book, the other lying on the ground, moaning. He looked at the face of the prone man and recognized Lucas. He looked down at the huge open wound and saw Lucas' insides. Instantly, he felt a horrible nausea. He ran off into the nearby trees, fell to his knees, and bent over, retching uncontrollably.

In a few minutes, he began to recover. He knelt there, breathing in the night air, trying to clear his mind. He heard voices nearby and saw another fire and men sitting around it. They talked in animated tones punctuated by occasional curses. He looked more closely at them and could see that they were eating. The smell of food brought on another surge of nausea.

The men wore broad-brimmed hats, and several had swords. One man walked among the group carrying plates of food. He was not dressed in uniform like the others, and his skin was black.

The dark-skinned man picked up a platter and walked to the edge of the group. He tossed something into the night, which landed twenty feet from Jason. Something in Jason told him that he needed to see what it was. He walked over to the spot but found nothing but garbage, the remnants of the men's meal.

Something about the pile of garbage sparked a thought in Jason's mind. He got down on his knees and examined the garbage closely. He saw the fragments of a skeleton. He grabbed a handful of the bones and examined them in the firelight. They looked like chicken bones. One of them was triangular in shape. It was a wishbone. He remembered the chicken bone that he had snapped hours ago.

Carefully, he separated the wishbone from the rest of the carcass. He held it to his chest as if it were a treasure. He hoped it would somehow be the tool of his salvation. He hurriedly made his way back to the field hospital. He needed to find Lucas.

In minutes, he was at Lucas's side. The man with the book was gone. Lucas lay writhing on the ground, moans of pain escaping every few seconds from his lips. Jason placed a hand on his shoulder, shook him, and called his name. Lucas did not respond, but Jason persisted. Finally, Lucas opened his eyes, and his moaning stopped. He looked directly at Jason. There was the faintest glimmer of recognition in his eyes.

Jason took the wishbone and placed one end of it in Lucas' hand. Jason forced Lucas' fingers around the bone and yelled into his face, "Grab it, damn you, hold on to it." With the last of his ebbing strength, Lucas did as he was commanded. "Make a wish!" Jason demanded. He heard Lucas mutter some unintelligible words. "I want to go home," Jason screamed into the night and pulled on the bone. The wishbone snapped.

Lucas had the feeling of falling, of being surrounded by brilliant light, his ears filled with a rushing noise. The sensations lasted only an instant. Lucas opened his eyes. He knew where he was. He had been here before.

He stood atop a huge boulder on the summit of a rocky hill. The sky was blue, the sun was bright, and a cool breeze blew from the west. The only sounds were the calls of birds and the rustle of wind in the trees.

Lucas had been to this place many times, more times than he wanted to remember. Every time he found himself on this spot, Lucas pondered the irony of his situation. Of all the places on the Gettysburg battlefield, there was no place closer to heaven than this stone atop the big rocky hill. But for Jason, heaven was an infinity away. He knew that he stood upon the summit of hell, his own personal hell.

He sat down on the rock as he had sat many times before, his soul filled with resignation and despair. He stared at the trees on the distant ridge to the west and remembered.

He thought back to that time over a century ago when he last inhabited a world that he could understand. In 1863, he recalled that he marched with Robert E. Lee's army on the invasion that would win the war. Lucas and his comrades were near the end of the long column of Rebel soldiers. On the first day of the battle, he and his regiment were miles to the west and did not fight that day - they could only listen with dread to the rumble of distant guns.

He remembered the long march of the next day, mile after mile of dusty roads, the air warm and humid. The wells along the route had been drained by their predecessors, so he and his compatriots could not fill their empty canteens. Upon arriving at Gettysburg, he and his comrades were immediately directed to the south, and by mid-afternoon, they stood in a long line on a ridge west of the rocky hill. Big Round Top was the name of the hill but he did not know that.

Hot and tired, they stepped off toward the rocky heights. He remembered the Union pickets that blazed away as they marched. He remembered hearing the distant sound of battle off to the left as they continued east up the hill, pursuing the elusive Union sharpshooters.

Finally, he and his comrades stood atop the big hill. He remembered his exhaustion and his extreme thirst. He rested for only a few minutes, for orders came soon. He turned to the left to join the battle that raged a few hundred yards to the north. He and his fellow soldiers marched down the hill and into the valley between Big and Little Round Tops. There, they encountered the Union soldiers of Colonel Strong Vincent's brigade, waiting for them among the boulders on the slope of the smaller hill.

He and the other Rebels attacked again and again, and each time, they were driven back. He thought back to their final assault, to the desperate climb up the slope. In his mind, he again saw the flashes of metal along the distant Union line and the unexpected charge by the men of the 20th Maine regiment, bayonets fixed, urged on by their Colonel, Joshua Chamberlain.

Like most of the exhausted Confederates, he turned and fled in panic. He ran through the trees and the boulders as fast as he was able. But before he reached safety, a Union artillery shell exploded overhead, sending red-hot fragments of metal into his body.

He barely remembered the stretcher-bearers who carried him to the field hospital, but his memories of the pain and agony were vivid. After hours of suffering, he finally passed into what should have been death. Instead, he found himself wide awake and his body whole, standing on a boulder on the top of the big rocky hill.

The first time he found himself standing on that rock, he had been filled with wonder and incredulity. He had just died a horrible, agonizing death. In the last flickering moments of life, he remembered wondering if he would find himself standing among clouds and angels or among pillars of fire and laughing demons. To his amazement, after his death, he found himself standing on that boulder on the top of that small mountain in southern Pennsylvania.

On that first occasion, he got down from the rock and looked around in amazement. He heard no sound of battle and smelled no stench of death. He guessed that he had somehow made a miraculous recovery and that he had been left behind by his comrades, who assumed him to be dead.

His immediate instinct was to return to the Confederate lines. He saw that the sun was low in the west, and it was in that direction that he should have been able to find the Rebel army. He climbed down the hill, heading steadily west. He looked constantly around for signs of other men but saw none.

Partway down the slope, he came to a path that led in the direction he wanted to go. Soon, he was at the base of the mountain. The path came to a small stream which flowed from north to south. A large log lay in the stream. It had been cut by hand, the top flattened to make a crude bridge. On the far side of the stream, he saw that the path continued past a barn and some small buildings.

He put one foot on the log and tested his footing. The log was firm and steady. He stepped across and set foot on the far side of the stream. At the instant that his foot touched the ground on the far bank of the stream, he again felt himself falling and was once again bathed in brilliant light. In an instant, the sensations were over, but he did not find himself standing on the edge of the stream. Instead, he was back at the terrible field hospital, lying on the ground in agony, his guts hanging out of his shattered body. For a second time, he went through a long and horrible death, his body racked by agonizing pain and terrible thirst burning his throat. For a second time, he felt his life ebbing and wondered what he would see in death.

Once again, after his second death, he found himself standing upon the boulder at the summit of the rocky hill. Again, the sky was blue, the sun shining, and the air cool. The wind again rustled in the trees.

His reaction on this second occasion was much like on the first. Once again, he descended the hill, seeking the lines of his army. For a second time, he followed the path to the stream and stood on the log bridge. He hesitated for several seconds and then strode across. He found himself once more transported to the agony of death, his third, at the field hospital. After several hours of horror, he found himself standing for the third time on the rock at the summit of the hill.

On this third occasion, Lucas headed south instead of west. He came to the foot of the hill where the trees ended, and as soon as he stepped from the cover of the trees, he was once more transported to the agony of his fourth death in the field hospital of John Bell Hood's Division of the Army of Northern Virginia. After a few terrible hours, he found himself standing atop the rock that was now familiar to him for the fourth time.

A dozen more times, Lucas climbed off the mountain and sought a route of escape. A dozen more times, he was transported back to the bloody field hospital and the agony of his death. Twelve more times, he found himself standing on the stone atop the mountain, the sky blue and the sun ablaze.

Lucas concluded that he had been sent to hell, but it was a hell totally unlike that conjured up by any preacher. His hell was this rocky hill in Pennsylvania.

He found that this hell was also a jail. Invisible walls trapped him. If he tried to pass through these walls, he was transported to the agony of another death and then back to the hilltop. Over the course of a week, he mapped the walls of his jail. At the log bridge, he found that he could sense the wall by stretching out his hand and feeling his way, but only at a terrible price in pain. When his hand touched the invisible wall, it burned as if he had dipped it in molten metal.

Lucas eventually learned the borders of his prison. The stream formed the western wall. The wall followed the stream north into the valley between the small rocky hill and the jumble of giant boulders. In the valley, the wall left the stream and turned east. It followed the position that the men in blue held on the day of the battle. It then curved around to the south and then west along the base of the big hill, where the invisible wall again encountered the stream.

By staying within those walls, Lucas could avoid the agony of additional deaths. But he soon faced the second of his agonies - the agony of hunger.

While he mapped the walls of his prison, Lucas also searched for something to placate his ravenous and growing hunger. At first, he looked for abandoned haversacks or discarded rations, but he found no such detritus of war during his explorations. Occasionally, he found mushrooms or various types of greens and devoured them greedily. They never seemed to make him sick, but they were never enough to satisfy his constant hunger.

Lucas wondered if he was alive or if he was a ghost. Would a ghost feel hunger? He did not know.

A few days after completing his mapping, Lucas heard a strange noise coming from the north side of his hill. He approached warily and saw a man chopping a tree. It was the first human Lucas had seen since he had been imprisoned on the hill. Lucas called out to the man and approached him. The man was startled and lifted his axe like a weapon. Lucas halted and asked the man if he had any food, but the man turned and ran away. Lucas stood forlornly, watching him go.

In a few hours, Lucas again heard noises to the north. Peering through the trees, he saw the man he encountered earlier. A second man was with him, a man wearing a badge.

Lucas stood and allowed the two men to see him. They approached warily. The man with the axe pointed at Lucas and yelled, "That's him, that's the one!". The second man lunged at Lucas, catching him by surprise and wrestling him to the ground with his strong arms. Lucas felt something cold clamp onto his wrists. He had been manacled. The man forced Lucas to his feet.

"You're under arrest!" the man with the badge bellowed. He took a piece of rope and tied it around Lucas' neck. "Come along!" he ordered, and Lucas fearfully obeyed. The man pulled on the rope, forcing Lucas to follow him down the hill, and the man with the axe followed close behind.

They arrived at the base of the hill. The man with the badge led him north up the valley. Terror grew in Lucas' mind when he realized that they were approaching the invisible border of his prison. Lucas screamed and begged to be released. He pulled on the rope and struggled with the man with the badge. The other man raised his axe and brought its dull side down on Lucas' head. He fell to the ground, stunned.

When he awoke, he found himself tied to two long sticks. He was in a litter - the man with the badge had constructed it from saplings from the woods and bound Lucas to it. Lucas felt the litter moving, pulled by the man with the badge. As they neared the invisible wall, Lucas screamed and thrashed but could not break loose.

They crossed the demonic border, and once again, Lucas went through the now familiar but still horrible experience. Once more, he knew death at the infernal field hospital. After yet another agony, he again found himself standing on the rock on the crest of the hill.

After that, Lucas knew he must conceal himself. He could not bear to be captured again, to be returned to another death. He became wary and sought out hiding places that would conceal him. Fortunately, few people visited the rocky hill.

For weeks, Lucas wandered the confines of his prison, constantly wary of unrecognized noises and watchful of other people. He suffered pangs of hunger and sated them as best he could from what little he found in the forest. He took to hunting, throwing stones at squirrels and birds, meeting infrequently with success. When he made a kill, he ate the carcasses raw, greedily devouring every scrap of flesh and internal organs.

For a few weeks, the weather was mild. The nights were

cool, but the days were sunny and warm. Rain fell only a few times in gentle showers. But one day, that all changed. Dark, foreboding clouds rolled in from the west, the wind began to howl, and the temperature plummeted. Lucas sought shelter among some rocks but was pelted by driving rain. The boulders offered little protection from the incessant wind and the cold, stabbing rain. All night long, the storm raged. He huddled among the rocks and shivered through the long darkness. It was the first time he experienced the third of his agonies - the agony of cold. It would not be the last time.

When the weather improved, he fared better, but winter was definitely coming, and mild weather became rare. Jason spent most days and nights huddled pathetically in the inadequate shelter of the rocks.

With the first snow, his terrible plight became much worse.

The birds had long ago departed, and the squirrels were secluded in hidden hibernation. Few plants were still alive, and those that survived were often buried in snow. The double agonies of hunger and cold tortured Lucas day and night.

One day, Lucas sat huddled among his boulders, feeling the most terrible despair imaginable. He stared, unthinking, at the rocky ground at his feet. A thought came to him. He stared at a sharp rock fragment that lay nearby, a fragment he sometimes used as a crude knife to cut apart the animals that he killed. He picked the fragment up, looking at it with unblinking eyes. He felt the edges with his fingertips, searching for the sharpest place.

In one quick motion, he brought the sharp edge across his wrist, cutting deeply into the flesh. His blood spurted from the gaping wound, soaking the ground at his feet. He watched impassively as his lifeblood flowed from his arm. He sensed increasing cold and growing numbness. As his consciousness faded and he felt his mind going black, he had one final thought - what will I see this time? He fell forward, lifeless, to the ground.

He opened his eyes and felt horrible pain. He was back at the field hospital, a large hunk of his body missing, a burning thirst in his throat. A man with a bible was approaching him. Again, he repeated his agony of death. When he opened his eyes, he was again standing on the rock at the top of the rocky hill. The sun shone, and the air was cool. He knew that soon it would be winter.

He tried suicide two more times. The second time, he dived head-first from the tallest boulder he could find, smashing his skull on the rocks below. The third time, he drowned himself in the deepest part of the little stream. Again, the results were the same - the agony of more deaths, the return to the hilltop.

He did not know if he was actually alive, but he felt all the pain and suffering of someone who lived. And if he was dead, death did not provide the release that he was taught it would bring. He would not try suicide again. He resolved to bear the agonies of cold and hunger rather than experience the greater agony of more deaths.

For years, he experienced this pitiful existence. He became a feral animal, skulking during the day and prowling for food at night. Hunger tormented him, but it would not put an end to him. His stomach growled, but somehow, his flesh did not waste away. Cold penetrated his flesh; his fingers turned blue, but his limbs would never freeze solid, nor would frostbite blacken his flesh.

He speculated that he might be a ghost, but if so, he was a ghost that people could see. Once in a great while, he exposed himself to a passer-by to see if they would react to his presence. They always did. When they did, he fled to his hiding places to avoid being captured again.

He did not interact with people but became a close watcher of them. As the years passed, more and more people came to visit the rocky hill, sometimes in groups of ten or twenty. He would hide himself in the shelter of the rocks and trees and observe them from a distance.

He himself did not change. He seemed to grow no older. His body did not deteriorate. But his prison changed around him, sometimes dramatically.

On several occasions, groups of people came to the big hill and its vicinity to erect stone structures and memorials to the men who had fought the great battle here. Several of these monuments were set within the invisible wall of his prison. Hundreds, even thousands of people, would come for dedication ceremonies. Another time, a tower was built on top of the mountain. For weeks at a time, Lucas could not venture from his hiding places for fear of being discovered by the construction crew.

The most dramatic change came when a road was built on the slope of the mountain. Great machines ripped trees from the ground and shoved boulders aside to clear a path for a highway.

Despite the danger of detection these occasions were godsends for Lucas. Each provided an opportunity for him to hone his skills as a thief and obtain items that would make his bleak existence just a bit more tolerable. There would be numerous unattended carriages and other vehicles that would often contain workers' lunches or picnic baskets. On a precious few occasions, Lucas was able to filch articles of clothing that helped him in his struggles against the cold.

The most valuable objects he coveted were tools. If a workman left a toolbox unattended for a minute, Lucas would stealthily approach and make a quick heist, then retreat to his hidden places. In this way, he was able to obtain a few knives, a hammer, and similar useful implements.

Lucas was careful to not be greedy. If his thefts were too

great, men with badges would come and search the area. Fortunately for Lucas, these hunters were never perseverant enough to track him down. Most of the time, the victims of his thievery assumed there was a petty thief somewhere in their own group and would soon forget their loss. Often, people do not discover the disappearances until they are long gone from the mountain.

Decades slowly passed. Lucas' life fell into a rhythm. At best, his existence was almost bearable, but often, there were long periods of agony and suffering, especially during the cruel winters.

The number of visitors to the rocky hill constantly grew, and in many ways, this was good for Lucas. The trash barrels often overflowed with discarded leavings from these visitors. Their unfinished meals made feasts for the poor wretch. But the danger of detection grew with the size of the crowds, and Lucas spent more of his waking hours at night.

Lucas lost track of how long he had been imprisoned. At first, he carved notches on trees, marking the passage of the seasons. Eventually, the number of notches grew so great that Lucas ceased his record-keeping. He knew that decades must have passed, but he no longer wanted to know how many.

One afternoon, after several days with no food, Lucas was driven by his hunger to go foraging during the daylight. He found a place among some boulders that gave him a good view of a parking area while still offering concealment. But crowds were sparse that day, and Lucas soon despaired of finding relief from his pangs of starvation.

Just as he was about to abandon his vigil, he saw a vehicle approaching the road. When it reached the parking area, it pulled in and stopped. Almost before the vehicle came to a stop, the doors flew open, and two young boys leaped out, ran across the road, and began sprinting toward the summit of the hill. Two adults immediately appeared from inside the vehicle, obviously the parents of the wild youths. They called to their children to stop and took after them in pursuit. They were in such a rush that they did not close the doors of their vehicle. Lucas recognized a golden opportunity and acted immediately.

In seconds, he was beside the vehicle. The adults still pursued their wild children up the hill so he was safe from detection. A wonderful aroma came from the back seat of the vehicle. Lucas saw two plastic bags on the seat as well as a plastic box with a handle. He grabbed the bags and the box and fled to his hidden refuge.

Lucas had struck gold. There were two paper bags labeled "chips" - one made from corn, the other from potatoes. There were two round plastic containers with lids. One was filled with sweet, shredded cabbage, and the other contained hot, brown beans. Lucas greedily wolfed handfuls of each. And then he made his greatest discovery. He found a large object in one of the bags, warm to the touch and wrapped up in metal foil. Quickly, Lucas undid the covering. He could not believe his good fortune. It was an entire roasted chicken.

Lucas ripped the legs from the body. He barely chewed the cooked flesh, eating like a ravenous wolf. He could not remember when he had last eaten cooked meat. In minutes, he had almost devoured the bird.

Lucas felt a sensation he had not known for a long time. His stomach was full. He no longer felt a need to eat.

Some of the corn and potato chips remained. Lucas folded the containers closed, delighted that he would have food for later that day or even tomorrow.

Lucas sat among his sheltering rocks, staring up at the patches of blue sky that appeared through the gaps in the tree branches. He continued eating the bird, resolving to consume every scrap. He pulled the bones apart, stripping them of every piece of flesh with his teeth.

He was nearly done. He held a small bone in his hand, sucking on it as he gazed into the sky. The feeling of a full belly brought memories to him, and he thought of his home in Alabama, an eternity in time and distance away. He mindlessly chewed on the bone for a while and finally took it out of his mouth. He began to stare at it. For some unexplained reason, he began to think about his grandmother. After a minute of meditation, he realized why.

His grandmother had been a strange old lady. One of Lucas' neighbors even called her a witch, and not without reason. His grandmother was a practitioner of "hill medicine," forever brewing horrible-smelling teas and other concoctions for people who came to her in search of healing. She knew hundreds of charms and incantations that she said could bring good luck or ward off evil.

He remembered one occasion when his grandma came to his home for Sunday dinner. His mother killed and cooked a chicken for the special occasion. When dinner was almost over, his grandmother pawed at the skeleton, looking for something in particular. He remembered her finding it and holding it out to him. It was a small, forked bone. She told him the bone had special properties and called it a wishing bone. She told him to hold one end of the bone while she pulled on the other. "Make a wish," he remembered her telling him. He heard a snap and saw in his hand a piece of the wishing bone. His grandmother held a larger piece. He remembered his grandmother grinning idiotically, telling him that she got her wish. He remembered his father telling the grandmother that she was crazy. That was the last of the memory.

He had never believed any of his grandmother's tall tales or superstitions, but something told him he should make use of this wishing bone. Lucas put it carefully in his pocket.

For a long time, he pondered what to do with it. He knew that he would have to find someone with whom to share the wishing bone, for according to his grandmother, two must pull the bone, but only one would see his wish granted. He considered how he would find that person. He had studied the visitors to the hill for many decades, and his years of people-watching gave him an idea as to what kind of person to approach. But he did not know how he would get someone to agree to share the wishing bone with him.

Lucas' gaze drifted to the plastic box with the handle sitting nearby. He opened it and found six metal cylinders inside, cold to the touch. He pulled out a can. "Budweiser," it was labeled. Lucas began to formulate a plan. The beer was just what he needed. He could use it as bait.

So that was how Lucas came to visit the north side of the hill, searching for a person with whom to share the wishing bone. That was why he approached Jason and offered to trade the beer for cigarettes. That is why he lures Jason with his bait and offers him the wishing bone.

Lucas remembered his anxiety as Jason reached for the bone. He remembered closing his eyes, wishing the most fervent wish of his life, wishing for an end to his life in hell. He remembered the snap, the sense of falling, and the light. And he remembered finding himself standing there staring at Jason, the losing piece of the wishing bone in his hand. Again the Battle for Little Round Top raged around him.

His reflexes caused Lucas to dive behind the tree, and to load and fire his weapon. But as he loaded and reloaded, he did not think of the battle that surrounded him. He thought only of what had happened after the snap of the wishing bone.

This was not at all what he expected. It was not like the previous occasions when he always awoke in the terrible field hospital, his guts protruding from his body and agonizing pain racking him. He had never before found himself transported back to the middle of the battle. Most astonishing was the fact that Jason had been transported with him. Nothing like this had ever happened before. One fact worried Lucas - he had lost the pulling apart of the wishing bone. But he could not help feeling hope, an emotion he had not known in decades. Maybe this time, he would not end up in the field hospital and not suffer a slow and horrible death. Maybe, he prayed, things would be different this time.

But the battle was not different. The Confederate line withdrew as before, then reformed and advanced. The Yankees on the hill charged again with bayonets, and the exhausted Confederates fled, just like before. Lucas' desperate flight was once again ended by the explosion of a Union artillery shell. One more time, Lucas awoke in the little clearing filled with wounded men, his body shattered and his life ebbing. Again, a man came with a bucket and gave him a ladle of water, and again, a bearded man prayed over him from a bible. Lucas fell into despair, for he knew he had not broken the cycle. He knew he would face hours of agony, that he would die, and that he would stand once more on the rock at the peak of the hill, trapped in his personal hell.

Lucas lay there, moving back and forth between consciousness and blackness. He wished for the blackness, for it offered relief from the pain. On this occasion, however, he felt a new sensation but did not know what it was. There was a voice calling his name.

Lucas opened his eyes. He saw a dark form standing before him, a familiar form, that of a young man who kept shaking Lucas' shoulder and calling his name. Lucas realized it was Jason.

Through the fog of his pain, Lucas saw that Jason had held an object out for him. Jason forced it into his hand and wrapped Lucas' fingers around the object. The object felt like a small stick. Lucas heard Jason yell at him, "Grab it, damn you, hold on to it." Lucas followed the order. He heard Jason say something else. "Make a wish!" he commanded Lucas. Lucas realized what was in his hand. He held a wishing bone. He mumbled his wish. He felt a tug on the bone and heard a snap.

Lucas opened his eyes. He knew where he was.

Yet again, he stood atop the boulder on the summit of the rocky hill. The sky was blue, and the sun shone brightly, and the air was warm and still. Birds called, and the tree limbs were dappled with sunlight. To the north, at the Devil's Den, far beyond Lucas' sight, teenagers filed into a school bus to continue a tour of Gettysburg. A teacher counted them as they boarded the bus to make sure they were all there. To his dismay, one was missing.

Lucas sat down on the rock. He felt neither surprise nor great despair. Resignedly, he looked around and saw that everything seemed the same as on every occasion before.

He stared off at the distant trees and gazed upon the rocks and the boulders. He looked at the ground at his feet, then stared at his hands. "Nothing has changed", he thought. He knew that his unholy cycle would repeat itself again.

He tried to see into the mind of whatever god or gods had condemned him to this fate. But so many things had been different this last time. How could the ending be the same? He stared again at the branches of the trees. A faint, warm breeze stirred the leaves, rearranging the shadows on the ground at his feet.

Lucas felt bothered. He did not know why, but something

tugged at his mind. He stood and looked around but saw nothing unexpected. Another warm gust came up, gently rustling the leaves of the trees.

Something was different, he realized. The breeze was warm!

Every other time Lucas found himself standing on the rock at the peak of Big Round Top, the air was cool and blowing steadily from the west. This time, the air was warm, blowing from the south.

Something else was different, he realized. He held an object in his hand, a small stick. He held it close to his face. It was the piece of the wishing bone. It was the winning piece.

On all the previous occasions when Lucas found himself on the hilltop, he had nothing but the clothes he was wearing. There had never been anything in his hands. But this time, there was.

"What does this mean?" he thought. There had to be some significance. He stared at the piece of bone, realizing it reminded him of something. He thought for a long time, and finally, it came to him. The piece of bone reminded him somehow of a key.

Once again, Lucas felt hope. He did not want to feel hope, for hope had betrayed him time and time again in the past. But he was human, and hope was an emotion that could not be extinguished from his soul. He had a feeling about this piece of bone that he could not deny.

He climbed down the hill, heading to the west. He came again to the familiar path that led to the base of the mountain. He saw the small stream that flowed from north to south and gazed upon the log in the stream. He was at the wall of his prison.

He stepped onto the log, holding the bone out before him. He inched his way along the log, step by tiny step. He braced his mind in anticipation of the terrible burning feeling, but he did not encounter it. He was almost across now, the bone still held before him. He shut his eyes and took another step.

He felt that his foot was no longer on the log. He opened his eyes and looked down. His foot stood on the earthen bank on the far side of the stream. He had crossed over.

He stood where he had given up hope of ever standing. He turned and looked to the far side of the stream, to where he had been imprisoned. He stood there for several seconds, staring at the trees at the base of the rocky hill. Suddenly, he became afraid. The silent trees and the looming mountain took on a look of evil and menace. He felt something reaching out for him. He turned and fled. He ran up the path as fast as he could, running past the barn and the farmhouse, fleeing the unknown terror. As he ran, he glanced over his shoulder, fearing what he might see. But nothing followed him.

He ran for half a mile before he stopped. He gulped huge breaths of air, and his sides pained him. He turned to look behind him, but all he saw was the path, the farm buildings, and the distant hill.

He could run no more, but still, he pushed himself forward, to the west, away from the hill. Soon, he came to a road where he had stopped. Many vehicles were on the road, zooming by at high speed.

He knew from the position of the sun that he had been heading west. He had always tried to go to the west, for the Confederate lines were in that direction, and in that direction was safety. But he realized now that there were no Confederate lines.

He looked to his left, to the south. Alabama was to the south. He had no idea if his home existed anymore and doubted that it still did. He did not know what lay to the south, but that was the direction he would go.

He turned to look at the hill one more time. It did not look evil; it looked like a high place covered with trees. But he remembered it as his own personal hell. He turned south and started to walk. He would walk for a long time. He wanted to put as many miles as he could between himself and that hill. And so he left the Gettysburg Battlefield, never to return.

In a small clearing in the woods that had become a field hospital for Robert E. Lee's army, Jason awoke from a terrible slumber. He felt agony beyond what he ever could have imagined.

He looked down at his body, illuminated by the bright campfire. His shirt was gone, and there was a large hole in his chest. He saw the broken ends of his ribs protruding through his skin. Every breath he took brought a stab of fiery pain to his chest. With every breath, he heard a gurgling sound, the sound of air bubbling out of his wound. Frothy red foam covered much of his chest. Now and then, he was wracked by horrible coughs and would hack up pieces of something soft and red.

In his hand, Jason clutched a small object. He was not even aware of its existence. It was a piece of a wishbone, the losing piece.

A man heard Jason's cries of pain, an enslaved black man who had marched north with the Rebel army as a personal servant to his owner. He carried a bucket with him and had been going to each of the wounded men in the clearing, giving them water. He went over to Jason and spoke to him softly. "Would you like some water?" he asked gently. He dipped a ladle into his bucket and held it to Jason's lips. Jason drank greedily. The man asked if he wanted more. "Please, I need a doctor!" was Jason's reply. The man patted Jason kindly on the shoulder and went off to give water to other wounded men.

Another man approached Jason, a short and clean-shaven man who carried a book. He spoke to Jason in a concerned voice. "The doctor's already been by, son, but there ain't nothin' he can do for you. He says you will live but only for a few hours. You must be brave, my boy, and make peace with the Lord. Would you like me to read to you from the Bible?"

The meaning of the words sank into Jason's mind. He did not listen as the man read. He just screamed in terror. The man read a few passages, squeezed Jason's hand, and went to minister to others. Jason's screams pierced the night, a horrible, wailing sound. As the hours passed, his screams became moans, and the moans became whispers. By dawn, no further sound had come from Jason's lips.

***

The young man sat on a large rock. His name was Noah. He wore earphones and listened to music. He was bored. This was the last place he wanted to be.

The others from his class seemed to be having a glorious time climbing around the rocks of the Devil's Den, but then again, Noah observed, they were all jerks.

The battlefield guide his teacher had hired called the place where he sat the "slaughter pen" and had rambled on and on about a bunch of guys killing each other. But thank God the tour was over, and he could sit by himself and eat the pitiful tuna sandwich his mother had packed for his lunch.

He sat passively, eating. Then he smelled something, a sweet, pungent odor. He looked around and saw a man, someone about his age, standing ten feet from him. The stranger held a marijuana cigarette. He was holding it out to Noah. "Hey, man, you want some?" the man asked.

At first, Noah did not reply. But there had been few times in his life when he had passed up a marijuana cigarette, and this would not be one of them. "Sure, why not?" he replied. The man sat down a few feet from Noah and handed him the joint. Noah puffed on it, inhaling deeply. Within seconds, he felt the effects of the cigarette. "This is good", he told the stranger.

In a few minutes, the two finished the joint. The stranger reached into his pocket and pulled out another. "Want some more?" he asked. "Yeah, I'm up for it," Noah responded. The stranger lit the joint and held it out to Noah with his left hand. He also extended his right as if to shake hands. "My name's Jason", he said. Noah took the hand, shook it, and told the man his name. He took the joint. The two passed it back and forth, and soon it was gone.

Noah saw Jason reach into his pocket again, but he was disappointed. Jason had not pulled out another joint. Instead, he held a small forked stick in his hand. Noah recognized that it was a wishbone. Jason held it out to Noah. "Want to make a wish?" he asked.

About The Author

John Baniszewski spent 35 years working for the National Aeronautics and Space Administration's (NASA) Goddard Space Flight Center (GSFC) in Greenbelt, MD. In 2002, Mr. Baniszewski passed the rigorous examinations required to become a Licensed Battlefield Guide at the Gettysburg National Military Park. He has conducted over 3,000 tours since then. In the late 1990's, Mr. Baniszewski's NASA work unit had a management retreat at Gettysburg, and Mr. Baniszewski gave a guided tour to his co-workers. At the place on the battlefield known as the Devil's Den, one of his co-workers asked if he knew any ghost stories. He made one up on the spot. When he got home, for some reason he felt unhappy with the story he had made up, so he put it on paper, re-writing it until he was satisfied with it. Then, for unknown reasons, he wrote another one. Then another one. He stopped at twelve. He titled his book "Stories from the Devil's Den."

These are stories about fictional characters, stories not based on real people (with two exceptions), but stories that are set in a real place and inspired by real events. That place is called the Devil's Den. The event is the Battle of Gettysburg. These stories are neither peaceful nor idyllic. Most are quite the opposite. But most have an element of hope.

In the complete book, the stories appear in rough calendar order – early chapters are set during the battle itself (July 1863), subsequent chapters occur over the ensuing decades, and the final chapter occurs a thousand years in the future. There is no need to read the stories in any particular order. Each chapter has a primary character. There is no inter-relationship among the chapters or characters. The events in one have no connection with events in the others.

For a number of reasons. Mr. Baniszewski chose to publish the stories as short, separate books and to start with two of the stories. In Mr. Baniszewski's full book, the first story of this book is *Chapter 8, The Trolley* – The main character is Strauser.

In his full book, the second story of this book is *Chapter 9, The Sentinle,* featuring the vandal Eddy. The third story is *Chapter 11, Santayana,* featuring Jason and Lucas.